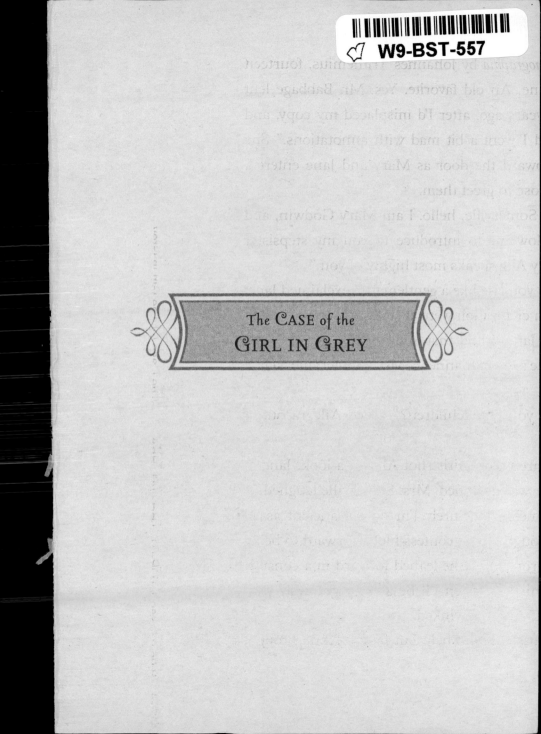

The CASE of the
GIRL IN GREY

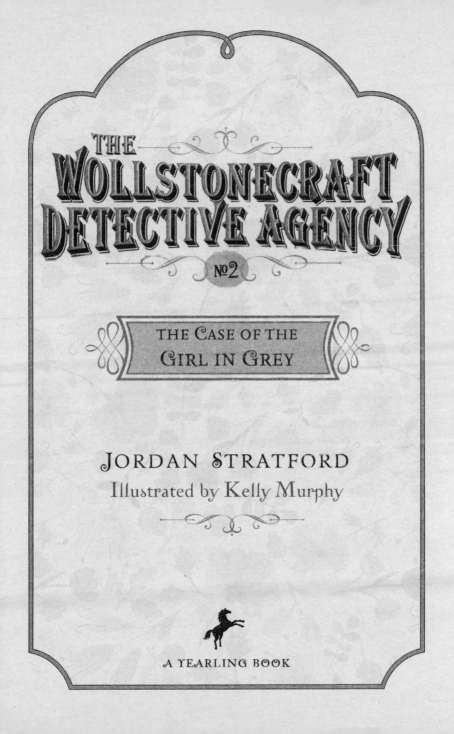

THE WOLLSTONECRAFT DETECTIVE AGENCY

№ 2

THE CASE OF THE GIRL IN GREY

JORDAN STRATFORD

Illustrated by Kelly Murphy

A YEARLING BOOK

Text copyright © 2016 by Jordan Stratford
Cover art and interior illustrations copyright © 2016 by Kelly Murphy
Chapter head illustration copyright © 2016 by Shutterstock

All rights reserved. Published in the United States by Yearling, an imprint of Random House Children's Books, a division of Penguin Random House LLC, New York. Originally published in hardcover in the United States by Alfred A. Knopf, an imprint of Random House Children's Books, New York, in 2016.

Yearling and the jumping horse design are registered trademarks of Penguin Random House LLC.

Visit us on the Web! randomhousekids.com

Educators and librarians, for a variety of teaching tools, visit us at RHTeachersLibrarians.com

Library of Congress Cataloging-in-Publication Data is available upon request.
ISBN 978-0-385-75444-6 (trade) — ISBN 978-0-385-75445-3 (lib. bdg.) —
ISBN 978-0-385-75446-0 (ebook) — ISBN 978-0-385-75447-7 (pbk.)

Printed in the United States of America
10 9 8 7 6 5 4
First Yearling Edition 2017

AMICUS EST TAMQUAM ALTER IDEM

For

Scarlet Abraham

Alexander Gryphon Bex

Penelope Brooks

Rose Hoover

Sagan Aurora Kilauea Oliphant

Sally Louise Standiford

Isolde Tan

Arden & Freya Teather

Cameo Wood

who were there ab initio

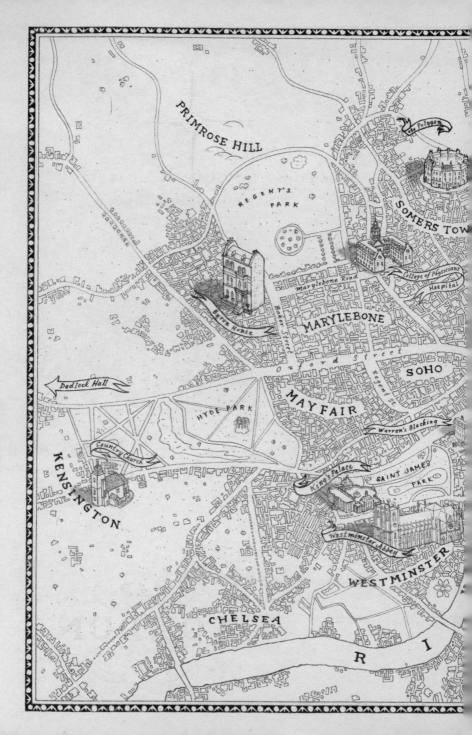

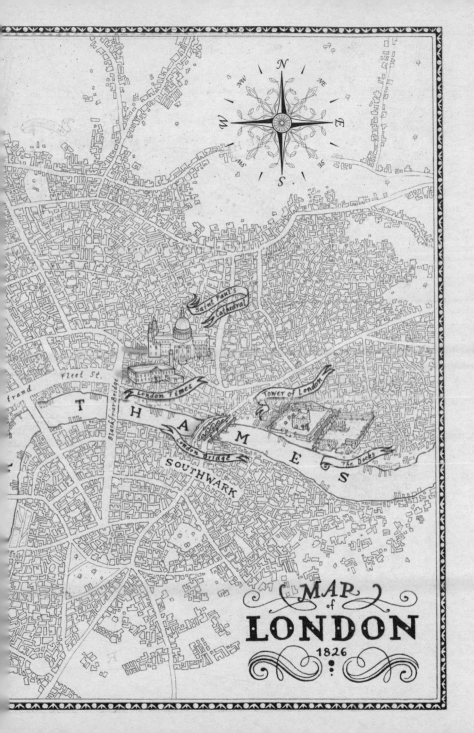

PREFACE

THIS is a made-up story about two very real girls: Ada Byron, who has been called the world's first computer programmer, and Mary Shelley, the world's first science-fiction author. Ada and Mary didn't really know one another—nor did they have a detective agency together. Mary and Ada were eighteen years apart in age, not three, as they are in the world of *Wollstonecraft*.

... that aside, the characters themselves are ... true to history ... we were sticklers ... At the end of this book, there are notes that reveal a bit about what is true and what we made up, so that you can enjoy the mystery as much as ever. We would enjoy knowing that you knew that truth was ...

PREFACE

This is a made-up story about two very real girls: Ada Byron, who has been called the world's first computer programmer, and Mary Shelley, the world's first science-fiction author. Ada and Mary didn't really know one another, nor did they have a detective agency together. Mary and Ada were eighteen years apart in age, not three, as they are in the world of Wollstonecraft.

Setting that aside, the characters themselves are as true to history as we are able to tell. At the end of the book, there are notes that reveal more about what happened to each of them in real life, so that you can enjoy the history as much as I hope you'll enjoy the story. Because the history bit is *brilliant*.

—JORDAN STRATFORD

DISARMING

1

"Did!" Ada growled through gritted teeth. She whirred the black iron coal shovel down through the air at her sister.

Nimble as a circus performer, nine-year-old Allegra pivoted on the stair just in time to dodge the slice of the shovel. She pressed her own attack up the stairs, lunging with her hooked fire poker.

"Did not!" shouted Allegra.

"Did!" cried Ada, knocking the poker aside with her shovel.

The two girls traded blows, one scratching the

paneling of the stairway, the other taking a deep chunk out of the white banister.

Allegra hopped back down one stair, then up again, thrusting past Ada's head, pulling back to use the poker's nasty hook. Ada raised her shovel over her shoulder to catch the hook with another clang and a puff of soot.

Poker and shovel locked together, the older sister flicked her wrist, whipping the poker from Allegra's grip, spinning it right around until it shot like an arrow back down the stairs to embed into the doorframe with a reverberating thud.

Ada leveled the shovel into Allegra's face in triumph. Quick as lightning, Allegra dropped to her knees, grabbed her sister's ankles, and gave a sharp yank. Ada's bottom spanked hard against the wooden stair. She started to yowl like a wet cat, the shovel skittering down the stairs and along the tiled hall.

The toe of a gleaming black shoe stopped the shovel's slide. Above the black shoe was a black-cuffed trouser of a long black suit, and very far atop the suit was the drawn and displeased face of Ada's very large, tall butler, Mr. Franklin. He said nothing, but his silence and his look of disapproval were enough to stop

Ada's wailing immediately. He folded himself to pick up the shovel without bending his legs, which struck Allegra as very flexible and Ada as a long way down, and rose again to pluck the still-trembling poker from the woodwork.

Embarrassed, both girls rose and coughed, smoothing their gowns and brushing the soot from their hands, making more of a mess in the process. Neither sister could entirely remember the reason for the staircase duel in the first place, "dids" and "did nots" gone in an instant.

The butler stared at the pair for a moment with a raised eyebrow, then slowly turned, returning the implements to the fireplace. The girls remained humbled for as long as they could manage, which was about two entire seconds.

"That was brilliant!" cried Allegra. "You have to show me how to do that!"

"The disarm? It's in the book. Agrippa, I think. Capo Ferro? Fencing books. They're in the library."

"You couldn't just show me?"

"You couldn't just read a book?" Ada replied.

"Honestly, Ada, you're mean."

"You're impossible," declared Ada, marching up

the stairs to the library. Allegra followed, although she pretended not to.

Ada found a book on sixteenth-century fencing and pressed it into her sister's hands. "Didn't you take a room?" she asked, still pushing on the book, prodding Allegra subtly toward the door.

"I took three, really," admitted Allegra, not taking the hint at all. "They were just empty."

"They weren't empty—they had things in them."

"Things under sheets," Allegra clarified.

"Things that weren't yours," Ada replied.

"Well, they're just rooms. And you have a lot of them."

Indeed, there were a lot of rooms in the stately Marylebone house in the heart of London, and most of them were empty, except for things under sheets. Curiously for such a grand house, there had been only four people living there: Lady Ada Byron; her silent butler, Mr. Franklin; the cook, whose name Ada really was making an effort to remember; and Miss Cumberland, Ada's maid. Ada's father, the notorious Lord Byron, had died on an adventure in Greece two years earlier, when Ada was nine, and her mother had taken to the family estate in the country. But she had not taken Ada. This had left Ada alone with the three servants. Alone, that is, until Ada's half sister, Allegra, had arrived on Ada's doorstep, taking over three rooms and never seeming to settle in any of them.

Until very recently, Ada's world had been a comfortable, sense-making place of books and ideas, of drawings and charts, of mathematics and puzzles, of machines and inventions and a hot-air balloon of her own making, tethered to the roof, in which to think. Then a month ago all had changed. Her governess had departed, a tutor had arrived, and a fellow tutee and friend with an appetite for adventure appeared. That was certainly enough change for one eleven-almost-twelve-year-old girl.

And none of that called for an additional sister.

Ada admitted to herself that Allegra was a most capable nine-year-old. She could read and write and juggle, she could do perfect handstands and even recite some Latin and Italian due to having been raised by nuns on the continent. But "settling" seemed completely beyond Allegra's abilities. She would fidget, or tap, or twirl at random, or run all the way upstairs and all the way down again if she forgot something.

Allegra was so unsettled that she unsettled herself all the way from Italy to England, seemingly for the sole purpose of unsettling Ada.

"You're only here until—"

"I know, I know," Allegra interrupted. "Christmas, when your mother gets home. I'll bet she'll have kittens when she sees me!"

"You think she'll bring you a cat?" asked Ada, confused.

"No, cranky-head. It means she'll go mad! I'll remind her of our dad, and she absolutely hates him. And me. Isn't that marvelous? She'll lay an egg!"

Ada loved words and tried to use them very carefully. She found her sister's jumble of egg-laying kittens unsettling. Here, in the library in front of all these treasured books, mixing up words seemed even worse than usual.

Ada really wanted to be alone, but it seemed that three almost-empty bedrooms was not enough space for Allegra to twirl about in.

"Never mind me—" started Allegra.

"I won't, then," interrupted her sister, more nastily than she intended.

"I'll be off to the circus soon," continued Allegra. "I ran away from the nuns for some excitement. And your detective agency is boring."

"That's not what you wrote in your letter," said Ada. "You wrote that you were coming here to be a Wollstonecraft detective, even though it's supposed to be a secret."

"It *is* a secret!" said Allegra excitedly. "That's why I wanted to do it in the first place."

"If it's a secret, how did you know? And how did Mother know?"

While Ada had her suspicions, she wasn't sure.

She and Mary Godwin had been entirely clandestine when they'd placed an advertisement in the *Times* to announce the formation of a private and secret constabulary for the apprehension of clever criminals. And they had used clandestine names when they pursued their first case. Yet a week ago, Ada had received a letter from her mother, the baroness, ordering her to shut down the Wollstonecraft Detective Agency, and the very next day, Ada had received a letter from her half sister, Allegra, saying that she was coming to join them. How did everyone know?

"Nuns!" answered Allegra. "Nuns know everything. They have some sort of secret nun powers."

"Nuns?" Ada was unconvinced. "You may have lived in a convent, but Mother—"

"Secret nun powers," Allegra repeated. "Anyway, I heard them talking about how your mother was going around the bend—"

"What bend?"

"*The* bend. About you and Mary playing detective."

"We weren't playing. We are detectives. We detected. We put a clever criminal in the newspaper."

This was true. Ada and Mary had solved a rather delicate case involving a missing jewel, a distraught heiress, an innocent maid, a phony fishmonger, and three men in red fezzes. The clever criminal was indeed in the newspaper, and he was also in prison.

Sadly, Ada's hot-air balloon had been lost in the apprehension of the culprit. Its charred remains (the balloon, not the culprit) were now on the bottom of the river Thames rather than at the top of the Byron house. Ada had been sketching plans for an improved balloon—but it wouldn't be ready soon enough to save her from her unsettling sister.

"In any event, you're boring, and you won't let me

be a detective, so I'm off to the circus. Straightaway after Christmas."

"We're not boring, Allegra. Mary and I are trying to help people. I'm the clever one, and Mary does people. Well, she notices things about them. It's not that we won't let you. I just don't know what you'd do."

"I can juggle."

"How would that help?" Ada asked.

"I'm very bendy. I've been practicing for the circus."

"We're a secret constabulary, Allegra. We don't need bendy."

"You never know," sulked Allegra.

GHOST GIRL

Mary Godwin was having sister troubles of her own. Her stepsister Jane was also determined to join the secret Wollstonecraft Detective Agency but vague about what she might contribute.

Jane had embarrassed Mary on their first morning carriage ride to the Byron house by asking Charles (the boy behind the book) why he was there, and if it was proper for him to accompany young ladies so, and if he was being ungentlemanly and (she stressed the word) *antisocial* by reading in front of them.

Charles, as Mary had expected, handled himself

expertly, although his answer was too direct for Jane's taste: Charles had no money for a carriage, and so he traded work for the coachman for a ride to work, which gave him a moment's peace to enjoy his book, as long as he pretended he wasn't there and nobody minded.

"Which we don't," Mary assured. "Mind, that is. Not at all."

Jane had further embarrassed Mary by insisting on calling Charles "Master Dickens," something Mary then realized she ought to have been doing all along.

After the first week of carriage rides, Jane had settled into the routine, and aside from what struck Mary as an overly formal "Good morning," Jane had kept largely to herself, immersed in her own book. The carriage turned from their home on Polygon Road down Eversholt Street, seemingly in the wrong direction, only to turn again the right way some minutes later. This turn took them toward the outer circle of Regent's Park proper, its manicured green all around them.

Without warning, the carriage rocked back, bucking the girls nearly into Charles's lap, and Mary's knee landed hard on the rough wooden planks. The horses cried out in front, hooves hammering the autumn-wet road.

"Are you both unhurt?" asked Charles, offering a hand. As they nodded and righted themselves, Mary opened the carriage door to see what was the matter, and in the grey of the sky and the road and the rain, she caught a glimpse of a girl, perhaps a little older than herself, in a grey shift, soaking wet and shivering.

"It's a madwoman!" shouted the coachman in the rain. "She ran in front of us like the devil were on her heels! Nearly ran 'er to 'er death, we did!" Mary didn't hesitate to shoot after her, with Charles not long behind—but another carriage bolted past, cutting him off from Mary's pursuit.

The grey girl fled alongside a hedge bordering an important-looking building of white stone before disappearing into some trees. Mary ran after her until all was a blur: the green hedge, the white stone, the grey girl.

"Wait!" shouted Mary at the vanishing girl. "Are you all right?"

Mary leaned a gloved hand against a tree to catch her breath. A pale-faced girl peered out from behind another tree a short distance on, auburn hair tangled and rain-pasted to her cheeks.

"I say," panted Mary, "I do hope you're all right. You've had a bit of a fright, I should think."

"No," replied the girl, as though from a great distance. "I'm not all right." There was a strange, otherworldly note in her voice.

Mary was alarmed. "Was it the horses? Were you hurt?"

"No," came the reply. "It wasn't the horses. I'm just not all right."

"Please do come back to the carriage. Out of the rain. You're soaked through. We can take you home."

"I'm not all right," said the girl in grey. "And I'm not going home." With that, she turned an even whiter shade of pale and fled into the trees alongside the path, quick as a bird.

Mystified by the disappearing girl's odd behavior, Mary was unsure of what to do. She turned to see Charles, just catching up.

"Miss Godwin? Are you altogether well?" he inquired. "You look as if you've seen a ghost."

"Perhaps I have, Master Dickens." Mary adjusted her bonnet and pulled her cape against the rain as she gave Charles a nod of thanks. "Perhaps I have."

TRITHEMIUS

3

Up in the library, burrowed in a book, Ada heard the lion's-head knocker, the sounds of doors, and the fetching of trays: all the formalities of "visitor." Ada's list of approved visitors had a single name on it, and as she was quite sure that this name did not belong to whomever Mr. Franklin had deposited in the downstairs parlor, she didn't feel the need to investigate.

Until, of course, she heard a flurry of light footsteps on the stairs. Allegra was on her way to investigate, and Ada knew she ought to head her off.

Mr. Franklin loomed at the bottom of the stairs

in such a fashion that Allegra was unable to find her way around him. He blocked her path until Ada, relatively composed, was behind her. The butler then pivoted like a hinged door, directing their attention to Anna Cumberland, Ada's maid, as she emerged from the parlor. Anna smiled and bobbed a quick curtsy.

"Lady Ada, there's a Mary Somerville to see you."

Ada froze. "That's impossible," said Ada. "It can't be."

"You were expecting her. She sent a note."

"A note?"

"You read it at breakfast, Lady Ada."

"I don't remember it. I would have remembered it."

"You were reading something else at the same time," added Anna.

"I can do that! I can read two things at the same time and remember them."

"I'm sure you can, Lady Ada."

"I would have remembered a note from Mrs. Somerville!"

"No doubt, Lady Ada."

"Mary Somerville. The smartest person in England. The smartest, cleverest person in the whole world. Wrote me a note. I would have remembered."

"As you say, Lady Ada," said a patient Anna.

Allegra. The sister had entered Ada's brain like a mosquito in a summer night's bedroom. She was sure she would have remembered everything if her sister hadn't simply . . .

Allegra trotted into the parlor like a spaniel, not caring a bit who Mrs. Somerville might be or that she wasn't there to visit the younger sister.

Ada, in something of a shock, followed on.

A kindly-looking woman in a coffee-brown dress rose and extended her hand. She was perhaps forty-five or so, with a prominent nose and slightly slanted eyes. Her plain façade could not mask a ferocious intelligence, which Ada recognized at once.

"Lady Ada," said the woman. "Delighted to meet you at last."

Ada froze once more, star-struck. She blinked forcefully, and as this didn't help, she blinked again. The woman continued.

"I'm—"

"Mary Somerville."

"Yes, that's right. I understand we have a mutual friend in—"

"Mr. Babbage," Ada interrupted again.

Mrs. Somerville smiled, and her eyes motioned to the furniture in the subtlest reminder that they might all wish to sit down.

"Trithemius," Ada added, blinking yet again.

"I beg your pardon?" asked Mrs. Somerville.

"*Steganographia.* Fourteen ninety-nine. I have your—I mean—Mr. Babbage left—gave me—I—you—"

"Have I startled you, Lady Ada?" asked Mrs. Somerville, concerned.

Ada continued to stare at Mrs. Somerville, and Allegra stared at Ada, trying not to laugh.

Ada panicked and bolted from the room, leaving Allegra to hurl herself at the couch and begin chatting away at the now-captive Mrs. Somerville.

Ada shot to the library, found her quarry, and flew back down the stairs to find Mary Godwin, looking soggy and pale, in the foyer with the curly-haired and perfectly dry Jane in tow.

"What's wrong?" asked both Ada and Mary of each other at once.

"I'm fine," said Mary. "Our carriage had a bit of a start. Well, a stop would be more accurate. But what about you? You look a shambles. How did you get so sooty?"

Ada was still wide-eyed and flustered.

"Mary Somerville. In my house. Behind that door. Trapped, with Allegra."

Mary knew that when Ada began to chop up her sentences, she was feeling overwhelmed.

"Dear Ada, do calm down. Now, are you saying that Allegra has trapped some woman behind the door, and we are to set her free?"

"No, no. It's Mary Somerville. She's the smartest person in England. She's the smartest person in the *whole world*." Ada's words were racing. "Honestly, she's so clever, they had to invent a new word for it."

"What word?" asked Mary.

"Scientist!" Ada babbled excitedly. "They used to say 'men of science' until she came along. And I have her book—well, I have several of her books. The ones she's written. But I mean Mr. Babbage's book, well, he didn't write it—Trithemius wrote it three hundred twenty-seven years ago. But Mary Somerville wrote in it! And I read her notes! And there are things I don't understand! It's probably the best thing that's ever happened."

"Oh, well then. That's good. I must say, you don't look like it's the best thing that ever happened."

"Good grief," said Ada, remembering. "Mary Somerville is stranded in that room with my sister."

"Well," replied Mary, "Allegra is very . . . entertaining. Come now, there's no need to keep Mrs.—"

"Somerville."

"—Mrs. Somerville waiting. I'll be in shortly. You'll be perfectly fine, I promise." Mary gave Ada the slightest push as the door opened, then returned to the task of removing her cape and bonnet and trying to dry off.

Ada stepped through the parlor doorway to see Mrs. Somerville patiently nodding as Allegra prattled on about her various circus talents.

"I do apologize, Mrs. Somerville—" Ada began.

"My dear girl, think nothing of it. I know this is your house, but please do come sit down," said Mrs. Somerville kindly.

Ada sat beside Allegra, and this caused the younger girl to bend herself into a more ladylike position.

"It's just that Mr. Babbage lent me this book," continued Ada, handing the small brown volume to Mrs. Somerville, noting that it matched her dress. "You wrote in the margins."

"*Steganographia* by Johannes Trithemius, fourteen ninety-nine. An old favorite. Yes, Mr. Babbage lent me this years ago, after I'd misplaced my copy, and I'm afraid I went a bit mad with annotations." She looked toward the door as Mary and Jane entered, and she rose to greet them.

"Mrs. Somerville, hello. I am Mary Godwin, and please allow me to introduce to you my stepsister Jane. Lady Ada speaks most highly of you."

"Why, you rise like a gentleman!" exclaimed Jane, as though civilization were at stake.

"Miss Jane, I find that at a certain age, one may adopt one's own manner," Mrs. Somerville stated plainly.

"Have you grandchildren?" asked Allegra out of nowhere.

The three other girls shot Allegra a look. Jane in particular was mortified. Mrs. Somerville laughed.

"Goodness, no. Surely I'm not as ancient as all that, although I must confess I look forward to being old and crotchety." She leaned forward in a conspiratorial whisper. "Then I'll be able to get away with anything." And she winked.

The girls couldn't help but laugh. Anna brought

in tea, and they all had a cup and a biscuit, allowing Anna to withdraw before getting down to things.

"Now," said Mrs. Somerville, "I suppose you're all wondering why I've called you here."

"I'm supposed to say that," said Ada. "At the end."

"That is precisely the point, Lady Ada, and thank you," said Mrs. Somerville. "I assume that you four young ladies comprise the Wollstonecraft Detective Agency?"

"No," said Ada and Mary, at the same time Allegra and Jane were saying "Yes."

"Well, I'll leave you to sort that out, but I have need of some clear thinking, and Mr. Babbage tells me you're the second cleverest girl in all of England."

"Second cleverest?" began Ada. "Who—"

"Ada's terribly clever," interrupted Allegra.

"But Lady Ada tells me *you're* the smartest woman in England," queried Mary.

"Person. World," clarified Ada.

"Perhaps," interjected Jane, "if we allowed Mrs. Somerville to speak, we would gain a clearer understanding of how to be of service."

"Thank you, Miss Jane. This matter concerns my cousin's family, and I fear that my emotional attachment may have clouded my judgment—which is why I'm seeking a second opinion."

Ada, back in the familiar territory of facts and problems, was an altogether different person. "Very well," she said confidently. "Begin at the beginning, and let's determine the variables, shall we?"

The Wollstonecraft Detective Agency had its second case.

BURKE'S PEERAGE

4

"Well," began Mrs. Somerville, setting down her saucer and discreetly brushing a crumb from her lap, "as one advances in years, one accumulates cousins. And cousins of cousins."

"Second and third," offered Jane. "With degrees of remove."

"Quite right," acknowledged Mrs. Somerville. "I have relations by the name of Earnshaw, specifically a Mr. George Earnshaw, a widower raising a daughter at Dedlock Hall, an estate near Kensington, perhaps an hour west of London."

Ada pushed her chair back ever so slightly and closed her eyes as she listened.

"Widower," said Ada.

Nodding, Mrs. Somerville continued. "Indeed. Mrs. Earnshaw passed away shortly after providing Mr. Earnshaw with a daughter. In any case, some seven months ago, Mr. Earnshaw sent a missive to the family that he was in receipt of some tremendous news that made him extraordinarily happy, and that a proper announcement was to follow. However, before this good news could be shared, he was tragically killed in a carriage smash."

"I'm so sorry for your loss, madam," said Mary at once.

"Thank you, dear. Please allow me to state that the crash was by all accounts an accident—carriage travel can be extremely hazardous."

Mary and Jane shot each other a glance and a barely perceptible nod.

"Elizabeth—Lizzie to the family—is in the care of another cousin, a more or less uncle of hers, a Mr. Thorpe. And Mr. Thorpe informs me that Lizzie is engaged to be married to a certain Sir Caleb Gulpidge."

Without moving or opening her eyes, Ada said,

"Cousin, announcement, carriage smash, orphaned daughter, uncle, engagement. Carry on."

Despite the grim topic, Mrs. Somerville ventured a half smile at Ada's eccentric but clearly impressive methods.

"Lizzie is to inherit the entirety of the estate. Now, I do not wish to accuse this Mr. Gulpidge—I do apologize—Sir Caleb, of any wrongdoing. But given the mysterious announcement and my cousin's tragic passing, less than a year ago, well, my suspicions are aroused."

Ada remained motionless.

Mary cleared her throat, and Ada opened her eyes.

"Mrs. Somerville," Mary began, "it seems you are asking for us to investigate your own—if distant— family, although no crime appears to have been committed."

"Yes," admitted Mrs. Somerville. "I am not one to assume the worst, but neither am I one to completely disregard intuition. I have been visiting at Dedlock Hall, and though Lizzie seems satisfied with the match, I confess I find the man . . . well, suspicious is putting it too strongly. But I would like the benefit of another opinion. Anything I ask of Lizzie—well, here I am, an old woman by her estimation, if not the grandmother Allegra makes me out to be—I believe she is telling me what she assumes I wish to hear. But perhaps you girls, who are closer to her own age, would see things differently."

"Heiress," said Ada. "Fishiness. Fishmonger?"

"Doubtful," said Mary.

"Ah," said Ada.

After the morning's incident, and hearing of Mr. Earnshaw's fatal carriage smash, Mary Godwin was reluctant to get into another coach so quickly. But Mrs. Somerville had already made arrangements, and the girls were expected at Dedlock Hall that very afternoon. This was to be a social call among young ladies, and their investigations would have to be, and Mrs. Somerville underscored this, clandestine.

The girls' tutor, Peebs, had arrived as Mrs. Somerville's coach was departing, but he allowed himself to be cheerfully persuaded to excuse them from lessons so that they might follow her and pursue the case at hand. He was grateful to be asked, and to not be locked in the distillery cupboard, as he had been during their first case.

Lost in thought, Ada scarcely looked at Peebs as he handed over that morning's copy of the *Times* and handed her up into the carriage. But Mary shot Peebs an appreciative smile, and then they were away.

"A baronet!" exclaimed Jane, looking up from the pages of her book.

"What's that?" asked Allegra.

"A titled gentleman. Sir Caleb Gulpidge is a baronet. His fiancée, Lizzie, is third cousin to Mrs. Somerville by marriage. He's here in my book."

Ada was not used to hearing about people being both alive and in books at the same time.

"What book is that?" she asked, her attention surfacing from the broad grey sheets of the newspaper.

"Burke's Peerage, Baronetage, and Knightage," replied Jane. "It lists absolutely everybody worth knowing."

"How? Why?"

"It is a guide to people of Society." Ada could hear the capital *S* and cringed a little. "And yes," said Jane, who could barely contain herself, "you're in here as well, Lady Ada!"

"Let me see that." Ada held out her hand.

"Certainly, Lady Ada." Jane beamed. Mary shot her a look, but it was no use. Jane had already turned the page to "Byron." There Ada was, complete with her horrible first name, Augusta, and her father, George Noel Gordon (Lord Byron, deceased), and her mother, the baroness, Anne Isabella Milbanke. Birthdays and everything.

"Am I in there?" asked Allegra.

"No," stated Ada, finding the fact curious.

"Why not?" Allegra countered.

Jane interrupted. "We don't speak of such things."

Mary patted the back of Allegra's hand. "All kinds of simply delightful people are not in that book, I'm sure," she said with a reassuring smile.

Ada handed back to Jane what seemed like the most boring book in the world.

"What about *her* book?" asked Allegra.

"Whose book? What book?" said Ada crossly.

"Mrs. Somerville. You had her book."

"Oh that!" said Ada, excited now. "*Steganographia.* It's pretending to be a book about sorcery, but it isn't. That's the amazing thing."

"Sorcery!" exclaimed Allegra. "Wizards? Spells and stuff?"

"Yes, but no. It's actually a book about codes. It's just disguised as a book about sorcery."

"Ada," interjected Mary. "You're not making any sense."

"*Steganographia*," continued Ada, "is a book about codes—about making codes look like other things, so nobody even notices there's a code. And the book itself is pretending to be about sorcery. It's a book about things being disguised as something else that is actually disguised as a book about something else."

"I say, that's awfully clever," agreed Mary.

"Awfully confusing, more like," said Jane.

At this small rudeness, everyone looked out the window except Jane, who returned to her book, which she knew mattered even if Mary didn't like it.

"What do we have," said Ada blankly. Mary knew that this was a kind of question, and that it was her job to answer it, or at least begin to.

"Lizzie, a distant cousin of Mrs. Somerville, is engaged to be married to a Sir Caleb," Mary began. "Her father was to make some grand, happy announcement, but then he tragically died without telling anyone what it was. So there's a tragedy, and a mystery. And now there's to be a wedding."

"She thinks he's fishy," said Ada.

"Well, Mrs. Somerville thinks something's fishy. Because she doesn't care for him. Not much to go on, honestly." Mary sighed.

"She also mentioned an estate manager," said Jane.

"Mr. Brocklehurst, yes," said Mary.

"What's an estate manager?" asked Allegra.

"Someone who manages all the business of a great estate—the farms, properties, rents, taxes," Mary replied.

"Fishy?" asked Ada.

"We shall have to see," answered Mary.

The carriage rattled on in the rain, Jane purring over new Society connections in her book, Ada returning to the newspaper, and Mary staring out the window. Allegra daydreamed of striped tents and rings of sawdust, of juggling flaming hoops. But the long ride through the grey autumn drizzle and splootching mud squelched all thoughts of adventure. She sighed.

INCLEMENT

5

Mary gasped.

She stood stock-still in the gloomy grey-green front room of Dedlock Hall, pointing at a young, pale girl with auburn hair. "You!"

Jane was horrified. This was her first time in the home of a baronet, or at least the home of someone who was going to marry one, and her sister was behaving appallingly. As if she'd seen a ghost.

"Mary, do calm down," said Jane as calmly as she was able, which wasn't very.

"You," said Mary, still pointing. "In the park. By

the College of Physicians this morning. In the rain. Like a ghost. It was you."

"I can assure you, Miss Godwin," said Lizzie, a bit taken aback, "I spent the morning here, safe and dry, drawing."

"I can corroborate," boomed Mr. Brocklehurst, a boiled cabbage of a man. He was dressed well enough, in many layers of tweed, appropriate for a man who spent much of his time outside. "Lizzie is a most capable artist, and I passed her often to admire her progress." He spoke like a gentleman, though his accent suggested muddier roots.

Sir Caleb nodded his agreement, though he had gone a bit pale at the mention of a ghost.

"This is impossible . . . ," Mary protested.

"Obviously," said Ada.

"No, I mean, this morning. There was a girl in the road. It was you, I swear." Mary turned to her sister. "Jane, you saw."

"I'm sorry, Mary, but I saw no such thing." Jane was very proper in her manners in such company, and sounded very grown-up, if a bit snarkish. "I remained in the carriage while you dashed out into the road and then ran shrieking into the park."

36

"I wanted to see if she was all right," said Mary in her own defense. "We nearly ran her over. It was a girl, or a ghost, who looked exactly like you, Miss Earnshaw. But then she vanished, and she must have gone somewhere. Girls don't just disappear down rabbit holes."

"I'm certain," interjected Mrs. Somerville, "this is all merely a curious coincidence. The weather was most inclement." She looked at her audience and started to explain, "Inclement means –"

"I know what inclement means," huffed Ada.

"I don't," said Allegra.

"Indeed," said Mrs. Somerville. "Inclement weather is rainy, grey, foggy, and cloudy. This makes it difficult to see clearly, particularly after one has taken a shock," assured Mrs. Somerville. "I applaud Miss Godwin's sense of duty in the matter. However, we do not seem to be getting on."

Ada was unsure as to what they were to be getting on with. Mrs. Somerville had made it clear that their visit must be seen as a purely social call, and Ada had absolutely no idea what went on at such a thing. Social interaction was Mary's department, but even Ada could see that things weren't going smoothly.

Still, the fuss gave Ada the opportunity to take a serious look at the fiancé. He was pale and a little oily. He was young enough, she supposed, to be courting Lizzie, but he had the thin hair of an old man, combed over the top of his head to disguise the fact. He held his hands together as though he were unsure of what else to do with them.

Jane glared at Mary until she lowered her pointing finger. Mary swallowed. "You're perfectly right," said Mary, "and I'm terribly sorry, Miss Earnshaw, for calling you a ghost, and for pointing so. I do so hope you can forgive me and let us begin anew."

"Forgive you?" said Lizzie cheerfully. "It's the most interesting thing that's ever happened to me. And please, all of you, do call me Lizzie. Though perhaps I have earned a nickname just now."

"The ghost!" offered Allegra.

"The specter," countered Lizzie dramatically, and finished with a laugh.

All this ghost business failed to amuse Mr. Brocklehurst, who looked bored.

"If you'll excuse us, ladies. Come along, Caleb."

"Quite right," said Sir Caleb, snapping to. "Ladies. Delighted."

Mrs. Somerville had settled silently into a book. Jane ceased holding her breath. Apparently Mary's outburst had not ruined their introduction after all. Mary looked embarrassed until Lizzie rose to take her hand. "Shall we take a walk?" she asked.

"But the weather is inclement," said Allegra—pleased with her new word.

"We shall have to take a walk indoors," suggested Lizzie. "The house is enormous and has not had this many girls through it in a generation."

Ada was unsure as to how she had expected things to go, but they weren't going that way. The house smelled odd to her—not unpleasant, but not the familiar scent of home and books. Not hers. The thought of it made her arms itchy. The sound of girls echoed through the sickly grey-green hallways: Allegra's chatter and Jane's clucking and Mary's smoothing things over, with whatever comments or laughter Lizzie might contribute. It was all a bit overwhelming, and was not, as far as Ada could tell, advancing their investigation.

As the girls wandered through the upper floors, Ada was distracted by a half-open door, or rather what she saw beyond it. A series of leather spines, standing at attention, row upon row.

A library.

Feeling not at all guilty for abandoning the others, Ada crept to the doorway and gave a tentative push. Rows of dark leather spines upright against dark wooden shelves, and between them, a portrait. A young man with auburn hair, finely dressed, a backdrop of ships in a harbor, and a flag—Jamaica, Ada recognized. The young Earnshaw (for surely this must be he, given his likeness to Lizzie) had the air of an adventurer. A man who had sought his fortune and found it.

"Oh!" she said, startled to discover an elderly gentleman seated in a wingback leather chair.

"Don't shout so, child," said the man. "My nerves, you know. My nerves." From the quiet of his voice, it didn't seem he really had much in the way of nerves to be complaining about them.

Ada surmised that he'd been hiding away in the library for quite some time. He looked rather in need of dusting. In his once-fine clothes neglected into

40

shabbiness, with all the color gone out of them, he had the appearance and charm of damp newspaper.

"I was simply investigating," said Ada.

"Investigating the library. It doesn't do much. The books mostly just sit there."

"I see them as standing," Ada said.

"Don't be bothersome, girl," he said, although he didn't sound particularly bothered.

"Mmm," said Ada, scanning the spines.

History, history, and more history . . . Where were the books on science and mathematics? Where were the volumes written by Mrs. Somerville?

"Who are you?" the man asked in a way that seemed rude and bored at the same time.

"Ribbon," said Ada, wondering if she had remembered to use her clandestine name upon introductions downstairs, then remembering she hadn't. Bother. "I'm a . . . well, a friend of a friend of a third cousin thrice-somethinged . . ."

"Confound it, urchin," he said as gruffly as he was able, which wasn't very. "My nerves! Why do you bedevil an old man so?"

Ada wasn't sure what he was going on about.

"I'll be going now." She turned to leave. While the

old man was complaining, he didn't seem to be putting much effort into it.

"Miss?"

"Mmm?" Ada had caught sight of a certain familiar spine, and was just going over to make sure it was the book she thought it was, when the gentleman interrupted:

"Do have my idle beasts of servants give you a good lunch. It can be exhausting, investigating a library."

Ada simply stared. She could not imagine ever being exhausted in a library.

A HURRIED SCRAWL

The girls were easy enough for Ada to find again—she merely followed the familiar tumbling sound of Allegra doing cartwheels in the hall.

And there was giggling.

Everyone seemed to be getting on quite well. They were hide-and-seeking in the many rooms along the corridor, only to have the game suspended when some curio was discovered, or asked about, or knocked into by Allegra. Jane seemed over the moon, getting to play in such a grand house as though she owned the place. The Earnshaw girl had apparently adopted Allegra as some kind of mascot.

Not meaning to be rude was what Ada was saying over and over in her head. Mary would like that. It was a good thing to say when other people were having fun but you simply wanted to know things and felt it was time to ask them.

"Are you actually going to marry him?" blurted Ada. The four girls turned silently to Ada, who had sort of sneaked up on them. "Not meaning to be rude," she added, remembering.

Lizzie put her hand to her chest, and Ada wondered if she had to check to see if her heart was beating. "Sir Caleb? Yes, of course I'm going to marry him."

"Do you want to?" Ada asked, and it was clear she couldn't imagine the answer to be yes.

"Lady Ada!" exclaimed Jane.

"No, Jane, it's all right," assured Lizzie. "I suspect Cousin Mary—Mrs. Somerville—has put you onto poor Sir Caleb. Some kind of investigation."

Ada glanced at Mary, who looked as though she'd swallowed a bug. Jane looked at the floor and started to hum, while Allegra swallowed so hard, she began to hiccup.

"Oh, I know," said Lizzie. "The famous Wollstonecraft Detective Agency."

"It's not famous," said Ada. "It's a secret."

"Girls solving mysteries in London? What girl in all of England doesn't know of this secret constabulary of yours? I'm honored, Lady Ada," said Lizzie. "Truly."

"Hmph," said Ada.

"Well then," said Mary. "The cat, as they say, is out of the bag."

"No more cats!" declared Ada.

Mary continued. "The truth of the matter is that Mrs. Somerville has some . . . misgivings about your fiancé and asked us to *discreetly*"—she stressed the word—"see if there was any substance to her unease."

"What kind of misgivings?" asked Lizzie.

"She doesn't like him," answered Ada.

"Lady Ada!" exclaimed Jane.

"She did admit she had no solid basis for her intuition," smoothed Mary. "Can you think of anything that would have made her uneasy?"

Lizzie paused, lowering her voice. "Well, there was the dog."

"First cats and now dogs. It would be helpful if there were some facts in this conversation," said Ada.

"Lady Ada!" exclaimed Jane yet again.

"Do you have a fish?" Ada asked Jane.

"A fish?"

"If you had a fish, we could feed it to the cat in the bag, or I could simply smack you with it the next time you said my name," said Ada.

"A smackerel!" said Allegra, feeling clever.

"The dog?" interjected Mary, returning Lizzie to the matter at hand.

"Well, we were walking," said Lizzie. "Sir Caleb and Mr. Brocklehurst and I. And there was a dog, just a wee, yappy little thing—it meant no harm to anyone. And Sir Caleb . . . well, it did seem he wanted to kick it. I rush to say he did not, but I was under the impression he was about to, which I believe is rather much the same thing."

"You're making me dizzy," said Ada, sitting down. "So Sir Caleb almost-but-didn't kick a dog, and this made Mrs. Somerville suspicious?"

"Oh, I don't think I told her about the dog," said Lizzie.

All four Wollstonecraft girls gaped at this, and Lizzie turned a rosy pink.

She took a breath and said, "I apologize. I know I'm not making sense. I've been so very alone since Father passed. And here you all are. Your reputation precedes you, and I apologize for pretending that I did not know the purpose of your visit. But I have so enjoyed being among such amiable sisters. But as you are all extraordinary young women, and as these are extraordinary circumstances, there is quite enough extraordinariness in the room, and I shall try to make matters plain."

"I think you need to try harder," said Allegra.

"Indeed, and noted," said Lizzie. "I imagine that Mrs. Somerville's misgivings stem from the fact that my father left me a sizeable inheritance when he passed."

"I'm sorry," said Mary and Jane in unison.

"Thank you. It was and is quite awful. He was a devoted father. My mother died when I was young, so we were uncommonly close. You asked just now if I knew of any reason Mrs. Somerville might distrust Sir Caleb. . . . I don't, as I haven't told her this, as it occurred just this morning so she couldn't—"

"Plainer," interrupted Ada.

"Indeed. Well, since my father's passing, my fortunes have been managed by my uncle, Mr. Thorpe—"

"The library," Ada guessed.

"Yes, he rarely leaves it. Anyway, he is running things until I come of age or until I marry."

"Sir Caleb Gulpidge," said Ada.

"Well done, Ada!" whispered Mary. Ada was generally not good with names. She'd only just learned the name of her own maid, who lived with her, so recalling the name of a gentleman Ada had just met seemed quite an accomplishment.

"He was in Jane's book," said Ada. Ada was good at remembering things in books.

"Well, here is the odd thing," explained Lizzie. "Mr. Brocklehurst and my uncle have always seemed in agreement about the management of the estate, and it was they who introduced me to Sir Caleb. But just this morning, Mr. Brocklehurst suggested that I should sign my fortunes over to Sir Caleb now, in advance of the wedding. He had paperwork already drafted for me to sign. And he became extremely put out when I refused to do so."

"But," asked Jane, "won't your fortune become his after you marry anyway?"

"Yes, of course. Which is part of why it didn't seem proper," said Lizzie.

Ada was getting a headache. There were so many variables floating about, it was getting crowded in her head. "Paper," she said. "Ink." Ada closed her eyes and held out a hand.

Mary fetched a piece of paper and a quill from a small writing desk near the window. The ink in the bottle was starting to dry, but its flecks and smears failed to distract Ada from taking furious notes. In the now-hushed room, all that could be heard was the scratching of Ada's pen. Even Allegra was momentarily becalmed. Finally Ada let go of a puff of air from her cheeks, which lifted her stray brown bangs in a wave hello to the dust motes in the air.

"Is that it?" said Ada. She thrust the paper at Lizzie, who took it.

The note was a hurried scrawl.

1. Mrs. Somerville (smartest person in whole world) cousin-something to Lizzie.

2. Lizzie rich or about to be. Parents both deceased (means dead).

3. Uncle Library (Gorp? Dorp?) employer of estate manager. Somebody. Broccoli?

4. Broccoli friend of Sir Caleb. Sir Caleb engaged to Lizzie.

5. ~~Caleb kicks dogs~~

6. Broccoli wants Sir Caleb to have Lizzie's money before wedding.

7. Lizzie won't sign money over. Broccoli mad at this.

8. Third stair squeaks.

"Well," said Lizzie, "that is the sum of things. It does seem rather plain, presented thus. Although it's Thorpe, not Gorp, and Brocklehurst, not Broccoli. But yes, you have the matter." She seemed sad, as though this simple note confirmed her heart's worst fears. "It is suspicious, isn't it?" she asked. Then—"The third stair squeaks?"

"It does," answered Ada.

"Is that important?"

"Just annoying," said Ada. "What if you don't marry him?"

"I'm afraid it's not so simple as all of that," answered Lizzie. Jane sighed and rolled her eyes at Ada's failure to grasp the intricacies of Society, but Ada shot her a dirty look, so she stopped.

Lizzie continued. "Sir Caleb is a good match."

"A baronet," Jane chimed in, and was relieved that Ada had no more unpleasant looks for her.

"Certainly," continued Lizzie. "He has been chosen by my uncle, and I have accepted him. The whole matter is entirely settled."

Mary entered the fray. "But why would Mr. Brocklehurst be so eager to have you sign over the inheritance before the wedding?"

"What if there was no wedding?" Ada asked.

Lizzie looked hurt.

"Well, honestly," Ada continued. "If you'd signed that paper, he'd have the money now and he wouldn't have to marry you."

"But think of the scandal!" said Jane.

"What if he didn't?" said Ada. "What if he didn't

think of the scandal, or didn't care about the scandal, and took all the money away and left England and never came back?"

Lizzie was visibly upset at this. "Lady Ada, I do thank you for your concern. But Sir Caleb is my fiancé, and we really mustn't slander him in this way. It wasn't he who suggested I sign over the estate but Mr. Brocklehurst."

The silence proved Lizzie right. The girls knew they had taken this all too far, and supposed a man to be horrid when they had no real reason to assume so. Guiltily, they looked at the carpet and mumbled apologies.

"Come now," said Lizzie, attempting to cheer them all up. "Here we have in our midst the second cleverest girl in all of England—"

"Second?" said Ada.

"What I mean to say is, this is no way to entertain such lovely and rare company. I suggest we go downstairs and play snapdragons."

Mary regained her cheerfulness, and Allegra could barely contain herself at the thought of both sweets and fire. Jane too was mollified by Lizzie's graciousness.

Only Ada seemed unrelieved.

"Second cleverest?" she asked under her breath.

SNAPDRAGONS

7

Downstairs, a silver serving dish had been half filled with brandy. Into the sticky syrup were placed grapes and sugared plums, and the odd raisin, before the brandy was set on fire. The girls all dared one another to dart their fingers into the flames to pluck out the sweets. If you were quick enough and brave, you could snatch a still-flaming plum from the dish; the fruit's flame always burned up and away from your fingers, looking much more dangerous than it actually was. Half the time, though, the girls would shy away at the last second, splashing their treasure back into the purple flames while the whole table broke into laughter.

Ada felt dissatisfied. She'd had no chance to ask Lizzie what the mysterious announcement might have been, and now they were too busy playing games to talk about the case. She left the table in search of Mrs. Somerville and hopefully some answers.

Down yet another grey-green corridor, past ranks of windows made of small squares of what looked to Ada like bottle glass, was the side parlor where the men, Sir Caleb and Mr. Bricabrac (Ada tried and failed to remember his name), sat smoking.

"Lady Ada," said Mr. Brocklehurst, rising like a pumpkin from the patch.

"I was looking for Mrs. Somerville."

"Ah yes, Mrs. Somerville. She was called away—rather urgent business, I think it was," he replied. "She left only moments ago by carriage. I'm sure she would have conveyed her goodbyes had it not been so urgent."

"That's . . . odd."

Sir Caleb didn't stand but merely sat there with his pipe, a scattering of papers in his hand. Mr. Brocklehurst's bushy eyebrows looked as though they were going to go over by themselves and strangle the baronet, so Sir Caleb hopped to his feet obediently.

"Lady Ada," he said with a bow. "I do apologize. Lost in thought, it seems."

"It seems," repeated Ada, unsure as to exactly why. She caught herself staring at them intently, squeezing her own eyebrows together in hopes that some sort of clue would pop out of them. It didn't.

She turned without proper goodbyes, which was just as well to Mr. Brocklehurst and Sir Caleb, who went back to what they were doing. Ada retraced her steps to the game. The fire was out now, a strong silver lid having been placed over the whole works and then removed to reveal the warm, sticky sweets beneath. Ada hesitated to join them, remaining outside the room.

Mary caught sight of Ada hovering there and excused herself to join her in the hallway.

"Mrs. Somerville is gone," said Ada in hushed tones.

"What? When? Why?"

"Exactly. I don't know if I can do this," said Ada.

"Do what, dear Ada?" asked Mary, concerned.

"Sisters. Yours. Mine. Them. All of it."

"They do make matters rather less . . . clandestine," Mary agreed.

"It took me all afternoon to get four facts from Lizzie. Jane won't stop interrupting with all her Society blather, and Allegra . . . I want to shoot her out of a cannon."

"I think she'd rather enjoy that, to be honest," said Mary.

"She probably would. It'll be her birthday present."

Mary watched Ada's frown turn into a modest smile at the thought of it, then took her hand.

Mary's eyes widened at Ada in a silent *sssh!* as Lizzie approached. Jane and Allegra had moved on from snapdragons and had procured a deck of playing cards from somewhere.

"I'm sorry, I don't mean to intrude," said Lizzie. "I wanted to speak with Lady Ada, if that's all right."

"Certainly," said Mary politely, who curtsied before joining the others.

Ada paused for a heartbeat, then blurted, "The announcement."

"I'm sorry?" said Lizzie, confused.

"Your father was going to make some happy announcement, but then he died. Do you know what it was?"

"No idea, I'm afraid. He didn't even tell me he was going to make one. It seems he sent out letters to the rest of the family but was keeping it as a surprise for me. I will say, though, in his final days he seemed . . ."

"Yes?"

"Grim. Troubled. I don't know. And then the—" Lizzie paused, the sadness she had set aside for the day returning.

Ada wondered what Mary would say. "I'm sorry," she said. That seemed right.

"You must think me awfully silly."

"Well, not awfully," admitted Ada.

"That's just it. I'm not silly at all. You've just caught me having a bit of fun, the first fun I've had in ages. It's because you're here that I can relax. I've been ever so worried."

"About the money, you mean."

"Yes. It makes absolutely no sense to sign away the money now when he'll get it after our wedding."

"Unless there won't be one," said Ada.

"Exactly. If he was so desperate for funds, why not just move up the marriage? We could have the parson around in an afternoon. Oh, I know it wouldn't be a proper Society wedding, but it would be perfectly fine nonetheless. But no, something's up, and I don't need to have Mrs. Somerville's brains to see it."

"No," said Ada. "You're not silly."

"And neither are you, so you know the next thing I'm going to say."

"Bubbleburst."

"Brocklehurst, but yes," said Lizzie.

"You think Sir Caleb may be an almost-dog-kicker, but he's more of a kicked dog, and not clever enough to be up to anything on his own." On saying this, Ada realized she might have gone too far. Lizzie graciously let it slip by.

"It was Mr. Brocklehurst who brought Sir Caleb into our lives. Brocklehurst had some business with Sir Caleb in Jamaica and brought him to my uncle's attention," she explained. "This is all some scheme of Brocklehurst's, I'm sure of it. Otherwise Sir Caleb would have asked me himself."

"And would you have signed?" asked Ada.

"Likely not. I'm still quite sure Father would not have approved the irregularity."

"I've realized two things," said Ada, thinking.

"What's that?" asked Lizzie.

"First, it's a lot easier to work on this case without all these sisters about."

"Indeed," said Lizzie, composing herself. "And the second?"

"You're *really* not silly at all."

An hour later, the girls, once again caped and bonneted, waited for the carriage as it was brought around to the front of the stately home.

Ada looked out across the grounds, to see a grey stone building nestled against the trees where the forest began.

"What's that?" she asked.

"Father," said Lizzie. "And Mother, next to him."

"What are they doing over there?" said Allegra. "I thought they were dead."

"They are," said Mary quickly. "It's a mausoleum. A family vault." There was no sign of recognition from Allegra, so Mary added: "A stone house for dead people."

"A crypt," said Ada. "Well, I guess that makes sense," although she secretly thought it a waste of a good stone house if you were just going to put dead people in it. As far as Ada imagined, dead people didn't really care where you put them. But she admitted to herself she really had no way of being sure. She realized she was tired.

Goodbyes were dispensed, and despite the whole visit being less than ideally clandestine, all the girls really had seemed to enjoy themselves. Despite

oddness and interruptions, Ada had the facts of the case, had met all the variables, and had found something of an ally in Lizzie.

Jane and Allegra both fell asleep with the bump and sway of the carriage, and Ada was tempted to join them in slumber.

At that moment, she desperately missed her balloon. Its creak and sway, its privacy and solitude, its view of Marylebone all the way to the park, down the nooks and alleyways behind Baker Street. While she could visit the roof, with its now-vacant network of chimneys and pipes and tackle blocks, the view would seem somehow less hers, less magical.

Ada sighed.

GHOST HUNTING

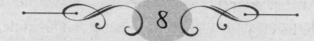

8

"The Peloponnesian War!" said Peebs with a grin.

The girls' tutor, making up for his students' day off the day before, hoped his enthusiasm for the subject would radiate through the drawing room.

Four girls blinked audibly. Mary was at least blinking with a degree of interest, and Jane was blinking uncharacteristically quickly, as though trying to force an interest that really wasn't there. But Ada was blinking "Why are you even attempting to teach us while we are in the middle of a serious case?" before returning to her newspaper, and

Allegra was blinking "What are these words coming out of your face?"

"Come now," implored Peebs. "Athens? Sparta? Democracy versus rule by the few, the end of the Golden Age of Greece?"

There was still no biting this particular hook. He tried once more in vain.

"It changed the map of the ancient world!"

Had there been crickets, Peebs could have heard them.

Ada didn't look up from her newspaper, but said, "How do you feel about . . . hunting ghosts?"

"I beg your pardon, Lady Ada?"

"The *Times*. This morning. 'Constabulary continues to seek escaped lunatic from College of Physicians hospital.' That's Mary's ghost, I imagine."

"That could explain the young lady's peculiar manner," admitted Mary, perking up. "Do you think this is at all related to Mrs. Somerville's case?"

"I can't see how, but it could put to rest one of the variables, at least."

"I suppose the Peloponnesian War will still be there when we return," said an only slightly miffed Peebs.

"A safe enough supposition, Peebs," agreed Ada.

66

An hour later, Mary, Jane, Allegra, Peebs, and Charles (who had been reclaimed from the boot-polish factory by paying a goodly sum to the foreman to give him the day off), found themselves in the well-manicured wilds of Regent's Park, behind the College of Physicians. Here, nature behaved itself. The trees had the decency to be all the same height, and the hedges were passable if you went about them the right way, with paths cut in on at-first-invisible angles to allow for the transit of gardeners.

Ada had given them all areas to search: Jane, Allegra, and Mary were to head northwest—a stroll of girls in the park was a rare unescorted opportunity; Peebs and Charles would cover the southeast part of the park and walk toward the center. Ada herself remained at the Byron house, fuming over her lack of balloon to oversee the whole affair. While she thought the connection between Mary's ghost and the Earnshaw case was tenuous, she trusted Mary's instincts. Besides which, she was grateful for the solitude.

"What, exactly, are we doing here?" asked Peebs.

"You know what I know," said Charles. "We're hunting a ghost. Or rather, a girl."

"And were you given more of a complete description of said ghost girl than was I?"

"Girl. Grey. Ghostly. Wet," answered Charles.

"Well, it's not raining, so that narrows it down to 'grey,' 'ghostly,' and 'girl.'"

"Auburn hair, Miss Mary said," Charles added.

"Did she? That's rather specific."

"Auburn is a sort of red."

"I'll have you know, young Master Dickens, that I'm quite in possession of the definition of 'auburn,'" said Peebs crossly.

"All right. Not everyone reads books, you know."

"That is an unfortunate truth."

"You wouldn't have read a book on ghost catching? Girl catching, if it comes down to it?"

"No," admitted Peebs, "although I suspect it would be ungentlemanly to write one."

"An escaped lunatic, Lady Ada said. Or rather the *Times* said," said Charles, making conversation. "Dangerous?"

"I suspect not, Master Dickens. I myself have given over to lunacy on more than one occasion."

After a lull, and a valiant search of a willow grove, Peebs resumed the conversation.

"And what is it, Master Dickens, that occupies you, if I may ask? Do you attend school?"

"No, sir," said Charles. "And seeing as we're together in this expedition, you should call me Charles."

"Charles, then. And I shall be Peebs, I imagine, as no doubt Lady Ada would wish it so. So, Charles, if not school, then how do you spend your days?"

"Boot-polish factory," said Charles, poking a suspicious hedge with a stick. "I glue the labels on."

"Ah," said Peebs. "That sounds rather . . . um."

"It is."

Charles stopped along the path. From the pocket of his woolen jacket he drew a small glass jar, like an inkpot, with a large cork stopper. He bent down to scoop up a small sampling of earth from beside the path.

"May I inquire . . . ," Peebs began.

"It's for Ada. Lady Ada. She asked me to collect dirt from all over London. Been doing it for a week now and just remembered that I haven't got this bit yet."

"Dirt? From all over the city?"

"She's sorting it, she says. Making a dirt map, so she can learn what color dirt comes from where."

"I hadn't observed dirt being in different colors," Peebs mused. "Actually, that's not entirely true. When I was on the continent, I had noticed the tones of the earth were markedly different there. But I imagined all English soil must be, well, English. Let alone distinctions within the city."

"I hadn't given it any thought either," agreed Charles. "But collecting these, I find there's all kinds of differences. Brown to black, sandy or muddy—it's quite beautiful, actually, once you start looking."

"I think that's marvelous," said Peebs. "It's quite the rage for young ladies to paint flowers, of course, or any kind of foliage, really. But our Lady Ada seems to be on a tangent of natural history entirely her own. Not that it's of much help to us in our current expedition."

"Later, perhaps," said a resigned Charles.

Peebs sighed. He was not overly optimistic about their mission, but he could see the logic in such a search. The day was pleasant enough for the time of year. Temporarily not raining, anyway. They continued along the path and continued in the not-finding of ghost girls. The grey sky took up the drizzle again, as dampness gave way to moistness and played with the fringes of wet. Charles and Peebs, footsore from gravel paths, admitted defeat, despite their reluctance to disappoint Mary. But there was nothing for it. Too much park, not enough ghost.

It might have been the subject, or it might have been his imagination, but a sudden chill took Charles, and the fine hairs on the back of his neck stood on end. He had the distinct sense of being stared at, though as he spun around, there was no one there to be seen.

THE SECRET LANGUAGE
OF CANDLES

Later that evening, after the disappointed ghost hunters had returned to the Byron house, and after an (actually) interesting lecture on the Peloponnesian War, Mary and Jane returned to their home in the Polygon building in Clarendon Square, Somers Town. The Polygon was a star-shaped building broken up into many apartments, and the star parts that belonged to the Godwin family were cozy parts, bookish parts, comfy-cluttered-homey parts, and good-smelling-bread-and-butter-and-cinnamony parts.

The girls set themselves to chores and chatted with

their older sister, Fanny, about her day, and helped Mama with the baby, which Mary preferred, or with dinner, which fell to Jane.

Mrs. Godwin—Jane's mother and Fanny and Mary's stepmother—was the most accomplished publisher of children's literature in all of London, but there in the steaming kitchen, flour on her sleeves and butter on her apron, she was more like a general commanding an army of obedient courses, with stacks of plates standing at attention.

"Mary!" called Mrs. Godwin from the kitchen, her French accent poking through when she stressed the *ee* rather than the *mare*. "Wash your face and fix your hair, child. A Mr. Hazzlit is coming for dinner."

It was the "a" that gave Mary pause. She was at a particular age: When an individual gentleman visited a home with a girl in it, and that girl was going to be sixteen at some point in the near-enough future, there was an expected sizing up or at least a looking over. As Jane was only twelve, and Fanny was spoken for, that left Mary at fourteen in the spyglass from a ways off. The whole thing gave Mary butterflies. Not pleasant spring-day butterflies either, of saffron and scarlet, but greenish-grey queasy ones that fluttered about her tummy. Their current case was not making the prospect of marriage look any more appealing.

Mercifully, this particular Mr. Hazzlit was practically ancient, forty something, although not as old as Mary's father. To be fair, Mary thought that in his day this Mr. Hazzlit must have been handsome enough. And his manner was sort of clever and vaguely grumpy at the same time, which Mary found amusing.

Jane at once prodded the poor gentleman to see if he was of interest but, on discovering that he was a mere journalist, quickly decided he was not. Her interest was piqued when their dinner guest let slip some name or other from Society with which Jane was familiar, and she shook the man like a terrier's rat until he let loose any crumb of scandal he could possibly spill.

"And do you write of the palace, Mr. Hazzlit?" Jane asked breathlessly.

"Alas, no, Miss Godwin. I confess I haven't the stomach for it. These days I restrict my reporting to the goings-on in the countryside and the waverings of my own moral compass."

"Our Lady Ada's been to the palace loads of

times," continued Jane, ignoring Mr. Hazzlit. Mary wondered when her friend Ada had become "our" as far as Jane was concerned. "She positively hates it. She finds herself so anxious among strangers that the thought of being at this table would send her trembling under it."

"Jane!" said Mary angrily.

"Now don't gossip so," said Mr. Godwin kindly. Mary's father did everything kindly; he had a kind face with kind eyes that sparkled when he spoke, and even his odd, blobby nose had a kindness to it that made it irresistible to babies, who liked to pull on it, at which the kind Mr. Godwin would laugh heartily.

The conversation took an adult turn onto the price of things, of stingy magazines and their reluctance to cover the modest and perfectly reasonable expenses of writers with regard to such things as jaunts to Italy.

"You should get yourself a patron, my dear Hazzlit!" said Mr. Godwin. "Were it not for the generous contribution of Mr. Shelley, we'd be poor as church mice, and the presses at MJ Godwin should grind to an unprofitable halt!"

" 'Mr. Shelley,' did you say, Papa?" asked Mary.

"No need to concern yourself with such things, my child," assured Mr. Godwin.

"Are you saying that my tutor, Mr. Shelley, is our family's patron?" Mary felt she had a right to know, although she couldn't say where either the feeling or the right had come from.

"He has been an admirer of my work, and your mother's," said Mr. Godwin.

"He . . . he has mentioned that," acknowledged Mary, remembering their first meeting in the foyer of the Byron house.

"Well, then, no more needs be said," said Mr. Godwin. Of course Jane ignored him.

"I do wonder if our Mr. Shelley is someone," she said. "I never thought to check."

"Of course he's someone," insisted Mary. "Everyone is someone."

"I meant—" Jane began.

"I know what you meant. Someone in your book. *Burke's Peerage and Sneerage.* Well, I'm not in your book—does that mean I'm not someone?"

"Girls!" said Mrs. Godwin sharply. "This is neither a suitable conversation nor a tone for the table."

Chastised, the girls nodded a yes-Mama, and Mr.

Hazzlit distracted them all by fluttering his fingers through the candle flame slowly without getting burned.

"I say, that's awfully clever," said Mary, holding baby Charles's reaching arms away from the fire.

"Candles are fascinating, you know," said Mr. Hazzlit. "There's an entire secret language about them."

Mary had her usual reaction to the word "secret," which is that it made her at once ferocious and invincible and feeling clever and in all ways marvelous. "A secret language! Please do tell."

"Well." Mr. Hazzlit, a natural storyteller, leaned in toward the flame. "They say that if the tip of the wick glows like a coal, that's called a 'sweetheart' and it means your true love is near."

Mary and Jane peered forward, but it seemed not to be the case. Mary felt slightly better about that, despite the vast gap between Mr. Hazzlit's age and her own.

"And if a spark flies from the flame," he continued, "it means a letter shall soon arrive by hand."

The part of Mary's brain that was growing to resemble Ada's silently asked how else a letter would be expected to arrive, by pigeon? She dismissed it and returned her attention to Mr. Hazzlit's candle secrets.

"Should the wick fold back on itself and fall into the wax, it heralds the arrival of a stranger." He waited a dramatic beat. "Or a thief." He had his audience in the palm of his hand at that.

"As the wax slips down the side of the candle, should it form a loop, why, that's a coffin handle and means that bad luck will befall the one it faces. But the worst of all . . . the worst of all is the 'winding sheet,' one fat, long drip of wax, meaning a horrible fate awaits the person opposite." His speech delivered, he smiled and leaned back in his chair.

"Opposite whom?" Mary asked after a moment of silence.

"I'm sorry?" asked Mr. Hazzlit.

"The winding sheet. Is it the person who can see it, who would be opposite the candle, or the person who can't see it, opposite the person who can see it who would be opposite the candle."

"Don't be difficult," sighed Jane.

"I'm not being difficult, I merely wish to . . ."

"My dear children," said Mr. Hazzlit, "I had no intention of setting discord upon this most hospitable table. I was merely sharing folktales."

"Please do excuse our Mary," said Mrs. Godwin. "She suffers from an excess of imagination."

"I'm entirely convinced, madam, there's no such thing as an excess of imagination." Mr. Hazzlit smiled.

Mary smiled at this and gave a confident nod in the direction of Mr. Hazzlit, who returned it.

Hours later, Mary and Jane climbed into the same small bed, knees knocking together in the cooling dark, with only a single candle to read by. Mary caught herself looking for a winding sheet in the wax and was relieved to find none.

Mary had settled into the opening pages of *Mansfield Park* and the fortunes of Miss Fanny Price as she settled in with Sir Thomas and Lady Bertram. Jane's cold foot nudged Mary's shin under the covers.

"Your Peebs is in here," said Jane.

"He's not *my* Peebs," answered Mary.

"As you like. Anyway, he's here." Jane pointed. "Percy Bysshe Shelley, born to Sir Timothy Shelley, and his father was Sir Bysshe Shelley, first Baronet of Castle Goring. His family goes all the way back to 1379 and the Earl of Arundel."

"Gosh" was all Mary could say to that.

"So what's a gentleman doing being a tutor?" Jane wondered aloud.

Mary asked herself if it was the right time to share with her sister that Peebs was a spy, sent on behalf of Ada's (and Allegra's, she supposed) dead father to keep them from becoming, well, too much like Ada's distant mother, the baroness. No, she decided. It was not the right time. And perhaps never would be.

This business about Peebs being her father's patron as well as a spy was unsettling and made it difficult for her to concentrate on her book. Mary's eyes were blurring in the dim candlelight, her novel and her own thoughts mixed up, and the arrival of the Crawfords at Mansfield began to impose upon her dreams.

———— ⚜ ————

Across London, Ada lay awake in the October night. She kept a candle lit in the glass lantern, as she had since she was a baby, and found its glow a comfort, enjoying the curious shadows cast by the clumps of drawings tacked to her walls and by the bits and bobs of machine parts that covered every flat surface.

When she heard the click of her bedroom door, Ada just sighed ever so slightly as a mostly-asleep Allegra tiptoed around piles of disassembled clocks and tools and stiffening tar-smelly goop in bowls across the floor. Allegra said nothing as she climbed in beside Ada, falling the distance to sleep she hadn't already covered, which wasn't very far.

Something had bothered Ada for several nights now. Her case—not this one but the last one, the first case of the Wollstonecraft Detective Agency, involving a mysterious pendant in the form of an acorn and a villain posing as a gentleman posing as a fishmonger, or some combination thereof. All had been settled neatly, with the innocent maid out of prison and returned to service, the pendant in the hands of its rightful Turkish owners, and a young heiress free to marry a young gentleman with a clear name, thanks to Ada and Mary's efforts.

And yet.

It didn't entirely add up, and Ada was at a loss to define how, exactly. She had mapped and sketched and diagramed all the variables she had encountered in the case, and all had been accounted for.

Except for one niggling, sneaking suspicion that eluded Ada's efforts at definition. A twitching hunch that teased her out of the corner of her eye, that darted away when her attention settled on it, like the half-seen tattoo on the fishmonger's arm. And there was the same certain unknown something about this case too, the matter of Lizzie and Sir Caleb. Whatever this something was, Mrs. Somerville had sensed it, and even her enormous mind was not grand enough, or grand in precisely the right way, to scuttle it out into the middle of the kitchen and squash it with a broom.

No, that's beetles, thought Ada sleepily.

Of course, she thought, grasping at waking before slipping into sleep. Remembering the spine of the book in Lizzie's uncle's library that had seemed so familiar, although forgetting, as sleep took her, why it was important.

The book was *Steganographia.*

CRYPTOGRAPHY

10

"So," Peebs coaxed from his small audience of girls, "after the death of Alexander the Great, the end of the Golden Age gave rise to . . . ?"

There was quiet for a moment, there in the Marylebone house parlor. The girls looked at the pages of Greek capital letters that Peebs had made for each of them: an alphabet beginning with alpha, beta, gamma.

"Rome," said Allegra, softly. All looked at her in a subdued amazement.

"What?" she asked. "I know loads about Rome.

Nuns were always going on about it. Lived there for a bit, I did, in between . . ." And she fell sadly silent.

"In between?" Mary asked.

"Trips," said Allegra. "Papa would come and take me on a trip for a month or two. Then wherever we ended up, he'd just, well, put me in a new convent."

"That's beastly!" exclaimed Jane.

"Jane!" chastised Mary.

"He'd come back," said Allegra. "Every year or so . . ."

"Well, it is beastly," Jane insisted, and Mary had to agree. Her heart broke for this little girl, who'd been played with and put on the shelf like a toy, to be raised by a new set of strangers after each adventure. Her heart broke a little too for Ada, as that same father never came back for her at all. Mary felt suddenly grateful for her bed, her room, her family, which had remained pretty much the same since her father had married Jane's mother, and they all stayed put together in the Polygon.

Ada wasn't listening. She was doodling over her Greek alphabet, knowing that she'd forgotten something, and that memory might be drawn from her head like ink from the quill. And then it was.

"*Steganographia,*" she said.

"Again?" asked Jane, bored already.

"There's a copy in Lizzie's library."

"Is that unusual?" said Mary. "You have a copy in your library."

"It could be the copy Mrs. Somerville misplaced before she borrowed mine, or Mr. Babbage's," Ada conceded. "But it seemed out of place in that library. And it is an unusual book."

"Your wizard book?" asked Allegra.

"Not a wizard book. A book about codes, disguised as a wizard book."

"I imagine," added Jane, "that having a wizard book—even a pretend one—would get you in more trouble than having a book about being a spy."

"A spy?" Allegra asked.

"Spies use codes," said Mary helpfully.

"I'd love to be a spy," Allegra said. "Or a wizard."

"It has nothing to do with wizards!" said Ada, beginning to get frustrated. "It's about cryptography, and I think it's important."

"Criptawhatnow?" said Allegra, not helping with Ada's frustration.

"Cryptography," said Peebs, "from the Greek *kryptos,* or 'hidden.'"

"Hidden writing, specifically," said Ada. "A code."

"But not, one hopes, crypt as in, well, crypts, with dead people in them," said Jane.

"Actually . . . ," began Peebs.

"Impossible, all of you!" Ada raised her voice. "Cryptography uses words or letters or numbers to stand in for different words or letters or numbers, so that outsiders won't know what you're talking about."

"Like our clandestine names," added Mary cheerfully.

"Yes. Well, no, not really," said Ada, although she was disappointed to say so, as Mary was at least trying.

"There are different kinds of codes," Ada continued. "One is to just take what you mean to say and jumble it up, and all people see or hear is a jumble of nonsense. But people might *suspect* that the jumble is really a code."

"Codes need keys," said Peebs "An agreement in advance, so that there's a way to unjumble the message when you're ready to read it."

"The marvelous thing about steganography—" Ada began.

"Greek again," interrupted Peebs. "*Steganos* means 'covered' or 'protected.'"

Ada gave Peebs a quick glare and soldiered on.

"The marvelous thing about steganography," she said, "is that if we agree in advance that when I ask if you'd like a cup of tea, it really means we're in immediate danger, then I could warn you without anyone else knowing you were being warned. We would disguise the secret message as a perfectly ordinary message."

"Oh!" said Allegra. "And if I said the phrase 'You're about to be eaten by tigers' really means there's treasure here and we should start digging, then no one else would know about the treasure."

"Don't you think they'd be alarmed at the thought of tigers?" asked Jane. "That's hardly a perfectly ordinary message."

"Well, maybe they would be alarmed, but then they'd run away, so when we found the treasure, we'd keep it all to ourselves," answered Allegra.

"Back to the point," said Mary, getting a little frustrated herself. "We know that Mrs. Somerville is aware of steganography—hidden messages—because she wrote in Ada's book. And we know that same book is in the library at Dedlock Hall. So I believe what Ada is saying is that if there is something fishy going on, it might have something to do with codes—codes hiding as perfectly ordinary things."

"Thank you," said Ada.

Although, as with Mary's hunch that the ghost girl in the park was somehow relevant to their case, Ada couldn't say precisely how codes might be involved—or what they might mean if she found them.

In her mind's eye, Ada envisioned a blackboard with half a mathematical equation. She'd need more numbers to fill in the equation before solving it.

But where to find them?

MUDDLE DUCKS

11

Ada sat in the guest bedroom in Dedlock Hall, her overnight bag on the bed, a bed much larger than her own, trying to remember why she'd thought it was a good idea to come. True, the other half of the equation—the part that was not already firmly in the blackboard of her imagination—was here. And she knew she was the one who would spot a clue if one existed. But she had suddenly remembered with some insistence that she didn't like to go out. At all.

The room was chilly, the coals in the fireplace doing little to warm the air, and there was an unfamiliar smell. She was a little put off by the amount of floor she could see—so unlike the landscape of books and clothes and bits of invention that cluttered her bedroom floor at home. The tidiness made Ada feel small and slightly queasy.

Her first night away, after eleven, almost twelve, years in Marylebone, and never a night at the home of a friend. She missed Mary and knew at once it had been a mistake to come without her. She missed Anna; she missed Miss Coverlet, her old nursemaid, gone for weeks now. She even missed Allegra and realized she must be losing her mind. Ada caught herself tugging at her dress.

There was a quick knock on the door, but even the knock didn't sound right. Fortunately, Lizzie's auburn hair popped around the door, with Lizzie under it, and Ada remembered that she did like her.

"Settled in all right? Ready to go for an explore?"

Ada nodded, hopping off the bed and taking Lizzie's hand.

"You'll be pleased to know that Sir Caleb and Mr. Brocklehurst suspect nothing," said Lizzie. "They rarely leave the drawing room, where they smoke and speak about who-knows-what, so I thought we might have a moment to ourselves. Where would you like to go?"

"Well, the library is a good place to start," suggested Ada.

"We'll have to wait. Uncle is something of a permanent fixture there. If you think there is something incriminating in the library, we'll have to investigate after he goes to bed."

Ada asked Lizzie to recount everything again from the beginning, and as they wandered the endless corridors of Dedlock Hall, Lizzie recalled how her father had seemed out of sorts before his tragic accident; how her uncle and Mr. Brocklehurst had found her a suitor, and how Sir Caleb had come to stay; how Mr. Brocklehurst had wanted Lizzie to sign over her money to Sir Caleb before the wedding, and how she had declined.

"Because he's fishy," said Ada.

"Indeed, although I suspect this is Brocklehurst's fishing and not Caleb's. And when I asked him . . ."

"You asked him?" asked Ada.

"I did. Why do you seem surprised?"

"It's just the sort of thing I would have done," said Ada.

"Well, that's good then," said Lizzie, pleased with herself.

"And?"

"And he told me that talk of business was unlady-like and should be left to gentlemen, and that I must trust him to know what is best and blah-dee-blah-dee-blah."

"Well, that could be fishy or he could just be horrible."

"Or just a gentleman confronted by a direct question by a young lady. That rarely seems to go well," said a resigned Lizzie.

The girls came to a side door that let out onto a garden path. The rain had given way to a halfhearted late-afternoon fog. Lizzie nodded the direction with her chin, and they continued speaking once they were outside.

"Perhaps," continued Lizzie as they crunched along the gravel path, "things will be different when we travel to Jamaica."

"Jamaica?"

"Yes, Sir Caleb has dealings in Jamaica. And we're to go there for a honeymoon, right after the wedding. Brocklehurst included."

"Do you want to marry him? Do you have to?"

"Yes, I do have to, or at least I think I do."

"Why?" asked Ada, not understanding.

"A young lady doesn't simply reject a baronet her uncle has decided upon. It isn't done."

"I'd ask why it isn't done, but I don't think you could explain it in any way it would actually make sense," admitted Ada.

"I fear you're right about that."

"Mary's mum wrote a book," said Ada. "Mary Wollstonecraft. She said girls should be able to do whatever they like."

"Wouldn't that be delightful?" Lizzie said with a sigh. "Perhaps one day it shall be so. I take heart in the successes of Mrs. Somerville, so I imagine the world must be changing, but how quickly I cannot say."

They strolled on toward the front of the house, and there, to the right and on the verge of the forest, was the stone house, the mausoleum, in which Lizzie's mother and father were entombed.

"Crypt," said Ada to herself.

"I'm sorry?"

"Crypt. Cryptography. Would you mind terribly if I took a look?"

"At the mausoleum? Whatever for?"

"I'm not sure," said Ada. "But I'm looking for something, and something tells me that the crypt is a good place to start. Have you brought pencil and paper?"

"I have, in fact," said Lizzie.

"Well, then, let's investigate."

The granite face of the mausoleum had two fat pillars carved out of it, with a triangular roof above and some sort of family crest at the center. Instead of a door, there was an ornate ironwork grille, like a garden gate, painted a gleaming black. Keeping the grille in place was a long iron bar with a latch. Ada unlatched and removed the bar and pushed the gate, which swung inward easily on well-attended hinges. She entered.

There were two long rectangles set flat into the stone floor—the resting places of Lizzie's mother and father—and around them a series of large letters carved into the stone.

"What are those?" Ada asked, pointing to the inscriptions, her eyes not yet adjusted to the gloom.

"Muddle ducks, I always called them," answered Lizzie.

"Why?"

"See? There's an *M,* and a *D,* and an *L.* Over there is a *D* and a *V* and some *X*'s. Muddle ducks. My father would come here, when I was little, and place flowers on Mother's grave. I thought 'muddle ducks' was an odd thing to put on a memorial."

"These are Roman numerals," realized Ada. "Letters that stand for numbers, from thousands of years ago. Used for dates, mostly. Years."

"Letters as numbers?"

"Yes. *I* is one, *V* is five, *X* is ten, and so on," Ada said. "Hand me that paper."

Lizzie did, and Ada took a moment to sit on the cold stone floor and jot down the deeply carved letters.

"That's odd," she said.

"What is?" asked Lizzie.

"Well, some of these have . . . dots, underneath, look," said Ada, pointing. "That *V* there is five. This *C* here, for a hundred, and this *I,* for one. Also, I don't think these are Roman at all, here and here. Also with little holes under them."

Lizzie leaned in, her hand to her chest. Here she was at her father's grave and felt both sad and anxious. Only her curiosity, and her marvel at Ada's, kept her from returning to the faint light of the garden.

"Look, see?" continued Ada. "This one here is Greek. A gamma, a Greek *G,* that looks like an upside-down *L.* And here at the end is a sigma, which looks sort of like an *E.*"

"I'm sorry, why is that . . . ?"

"Well, you don't usually see Greek letters mixed up in Roman numerals. In fact I'm sure you never see it. It doesn't make sense."

"Would you mind terribly if we returned to the house?" Lizzie was feeling too sad, and missing her father too terribly much, to stand there any longer.

"Of course," said Ada, seeing her new friend's sadness, and feeling a tiny bit pleased with herself that she had managed to notice.

As Ada stood, some motion caught her eye. When she looked up, she could see a tarnishing silver mirror set into the ceiling, overlooking the two graves. As she peered up, she saw her own reflection, staring down at her against the engraved stone floor.

MONSOON

12

Ada usually ate dinner alone. Alone with a book. She sat down and read a few pages, and when she looked up again, there was always a plate of hot food, which sometimes she would devour like an animal, if the book was exciting, or poke at absently with a fork, if it was getting to a dull bit. Recently she'd been eating with Allegra, whose table manners were scarcely better than her own. And of course she often had tea with the rest of the Wollstonecraft girls, whose manners were far more proper. Still, this was her first dinner "out," as it were, and she was a bit nervous. Jane would expect her to make some sort of impression, or at least make an effort not to embarrass herself too much.

"Jamaica," said Ada, interrupting Sir Caleb and Mr. Brocklehurst, who were murmuring at the far end of the table.

"I beg your pardon?" said Sir Caleb.

"Jamaica. I understand you have business there. What sort?" she asked.

"Sheep!" said Sir Caleb, at exactly the same moment Mr. Brocklehurst said, "Sugar!" just as loudly.

"Err, yes," continued Sir Caleb. "Sugar. I meant to say that. No sheep in Jamaica. Too hot, you see, for the, um, because of their, um, sweaters."

"Do sheep wear sweaters?" asked Ada.

"I wouldn't know. I'm in the sugar business."

"It's just," said Ada, "that you did just say 'sheep' when I asked you."

"It's the shushes. Sheep, sugar. Must be how the sound travels in the room. Erm." Sir Caleb quickly reached for a glass of water.

"It must be very interesting, sugar, in Jamaica," said Ada as innocently as she could muster. "Can you tell me about it?"

"Oh, it's, um, it's very difficult," stammered Sir Caleb. "You have to watch out for, um, erm, difficulties."

"I'm sure, Lady Ada," slithered Mr. Brocklehurst, his coarse accent grating on the finery of his words, "that the intricacies of commerce must be of little interest to a little girl. Shall we have some pudding?"

Ada did like pudding, but she did not like the fact that Sir Caleb was unable to answer any of her questions, and that Mr. Brocklehurst wouldn't let him even if he could.

As Mr. Brocklehurst reached for his glass, Ada saw a flash of ink beneath his shirt cuff.

A tattoo.

A single letter. *S.* And she knew at once where she had seen such a tattoo before.

She nearly gasped but covered it with a fake cough. She pretended she had seen nothing, and she was very, very bad at this. Desperately, her mind rummaged through drawers in her memory, searching for any subject, anything to say that might mask the fact that she was a detective, and was instead merely an ordinary eleven-year-old girl with no interest whatsoever in crime or suspected fishy characters or half-seen tattoos.

"Honeymoons. Girls like to hear about honeymoons, don't they?" Ada asked. Lizzie, fork in her mouth at that moment, nodded in agreement.

"The, erm, honeymoon?" Sir Caleb looked like he'd swallowed his spoon.

"After the wedding. I understand you are to sail to Jamaica and honeymoon there. I bet you've made all sorts of interesting plans," said Ada coyly. It helped for her to pretend to be Jane for a moment. "Specific plans."

"I, erm, well, yes, of course . . . ," tried Sir Caleb.

"What Sir Caleb means to say is that, yes, all the details are well in hand," said Mr. Brocklehurst. "But he wouldn't want to spoil the surprise for his bride-to-be."

"A surprise. How very thoughtful of you, Sir Caleb," said Lizzie, managing to sound completely sincere. Ada was impressed.

The house began to tremble ever so slightly, and a chill took the room. It was a familiar seasonal downpour, although to Ada even the rain didn't seem right in this strange place.

"I daresay," Lizzie dared to say, "it doesn't rain like this in Jamaica."

"I seem to recall that it does," said Sir Caleb. "Monsoons, I think they're called."

"Monsoons are only in southern Asia," mumbled Ada with a mouthful of pudding. "Jamaica's in the Caribbean. Different ocean."

Lizzie stared at Ada. Any hopes Ada had had about being seen as just an ordinary girl on an overnight visit were suddenly in jeopardy.

"We learned it at school," said Ada with her mouth still full, hoping that would make her sound less intelligent. It worked, although Ada knew Jane would not approve.

"Ah, well, there you go, then," said Sir Caleb. "School. Well done."

"Is Mrs. Somerville here?" Ada asked, after chewing and swallowing. "I thought she might be back."

"As we told you earlier, Lady Ada, she was called away on urgent business. In Scotland," answered Mr. Brocklehurst.

"Scotland? You didn't mention Scotland."

"Didn't I? Urgent business, regardless. I'm sure she sends her regrets at missing your . . . visit." There was a menacing tone hiding under his words, like a snake under a rug.

"Now if you ladies will excuse us," the estate agent continued, "we must go, as we have urgent business of our own."

At this Sir Caleb looked even more nervous than usual and stood up too quickly, knocking the table and dropping his napkin on the floor. He sort of patted himself down by way of excuse and apology, and nodded by way of a bow, and followed Mr. Brocklehurst into the drawing room to resume smoking. The oak doors closed behind them, and the house staff came to clear the plates.

"Lady Ada? Shall we?" Lizzie offered.

"Shall we what?" Ada was at a loss for what to do next. But Lizzie took her arm and led the way out of the dining room and toward the stairs.

"When you grow up in a house, you learn its secrets," Lizzie said. She placed a long finger on her lips and winked. Sneaking up the staircase, Ada strode over the third stair, avoiding its squeak.

"This way," said Lizzie, leading Ada through snaky corridors.

They came to a small, unused room at the front of the house, a once-upon-a-time nursery, Ada guessed.

At the end of the room were two large windows that overlooked a smallish steep roof.

Lizzie whispered, "Down there is the porch off the drawing room. They open the doors when the smoke gets too much inside, and they go out. We should be able to hear everything, but we have to be quiet!"

Ada nodded, and dared not touch the window lest some secret creak or rattle give them away. Lizzie reached out to the latch with both hands, giving it a push-pull-shimmy at the same time, and the window opened toward them silently. At once, the girls were splashed with loud rain.

"We'll be soaked through," Lizzie whispered again. "But we can have hot baths after, and get into our nightdresses. The wet won't give us away, and the downpour will cover any sound we make."

Again, Ada nodded silently, appreciating that Lizzie had seemed to think everything through. Lizzie crept out onto the roof, undaunted by the torrent, though the roof was slick. Night had fallen with a crash, and Ada hoped that she would not follow, to smash against the paving stones below as the rain did, landing so hard it bounced. Ada shivered, and hand over knee she crawled like a cat. A wet, miserable, cold, and unhappy cat.

Worse, it all seemed pointless. The rain made it impossible to hear anything but the mumbled voices of smoking men.

"What do we do now?" Ada whispered.

"Wait" came Lizzie's reply. The girls waited. Ada kept her mouth shut, for fear she might drown.

After forever, she heard the latch go on the glass doors to the porch beneath.

"But how can she know?" the girls heard Sir Caleb say.

"She doesn't know. She suspects. I imagine Somerville put her up to it." Ada was already squished together against the rain, but she squished even tighter at the sound of Mr. Brocklehurst's gravelly voice.

"She's just a girl," Sir Caleb insisted.

"She's clearly not just an anything. She's a spy, and we'll need to get rid of her."

"You don't mean—"

"No, no. The Byron child will be sent home in the morning. Then we'll need to move quickly."

"Honestly, I'm not sure about—"

"It's a bit late not to be sure, Caleb. And we're so

close! We even managed to get rid of your wife, before you lost her."

Lizzie jumped a little, and mouthed "Wife?!" silently to Ada.

"I didn't lose her. She escaped! But they'll find her, or the police will, and back to the hospital she goes. She's out of her head—no one will believe anything she says."

"You'd better hope no one will believe her. She knows too much."

"An escaped madwoman. The Godwin girl thought she was a ghost!"

"Well, at least Somerville is out of our hair for a while," said the oily, bloated man. "By the time she gets to Scotland and finds out there was no urgent business, we'll have you married, and the inheritance will be mine!"

"Ours, I think you mean."

"Of course, of course, Caleb. Slip of the tongue." His voice sounded even oilier than usual.

"I wish we could find that blasted will," Sir Caleb groused. "You know this estate—you promised you could find it!"

"I did find one! But he said there was another

squirreled away somewhere—thought he was being clever, but it didn't save him—"

"What if I marry Lizzie and the will shows up? We'll be back where we are now."

"A sight worse. You'll be in Newgate for bigamy."

"Listen to me, Brocklehurst. Find that will."

"Don't use that tone with me, baronet or no!" Mr. Brocklehurst spat angrily. "If it weren't for me, you'd still be losing at cards on the docks in Kingston!"

There was a strange, quiet tapping sound, and Ada couldn't make out what it was at first, until she realized it was her own teeth chattering in the freezing rain. She was shuddering violently, holding on to her arms instead of the roof, and began to feel hot instead of cold. Lizzie, herself a drowned rat, looked at Ada. "Are you all right?" said the shape of her mouth.

Ada nodded, or at least shivered up and down. She regretted it at once, as that shook forth a loud sneeze.

"What was that?" said Mr. Brocklehurst sharply.

"What was what?" asked Sir Caleb.

"I thought I heard . . . a sneeze. A girl sneeze."

"You're imagining things. This is hardly a night for a girl to be outside sneezing. She'd catch her death of fever."

"Maybe it's that Byron brat, or that wretched Lizzie," said Mr. Brocklehurst. "Maybe they're both out there in the rain, catching their death of fever! That would solve all our problems!" And the two cruel and deceitful men laughed at this, went inside, and closed the window.

Ada found to her horror that she'd more or less frozen in place and couldn't let go of her shivering arms. Lizzie was in the same shape, her skin fish grey and rain slathered. Ada thought she must have taken a shock by the news, by the words "wife" and "will" and "get rid of" and "death of fever," or by the rain, but Ada herself was getting dizzy, and it was awfully, awfully hot here in the freezing rain. *That's not right,* she thought. *That's not right.*

But Lizzie's gaze was not held by shock, at least not the shock of what she'd overheard. For as both girls peered out from their perch above the porch, they saw the ghostly figure of a girl in grey, as soaked as themselves, on the edge of the forest, there under the stony roof of the family crypt.

A STRANGER IN BROWN

The next morning, Mary looked up into the long, gaunt face of Ada's butler and felt a chill down her spine. The silent Mr. Franklin managed to convey a sense of dread. Puzzled, Mary nodded as he held open the door for her and Jane.

"Whatever's . . . ," Mary began. But the look of the rest of the Byron household stole the words from her lips.

On the stair, Anna Cumberland was pale as a sheet, her hand covering her mouth, and her eyes rimmed with tears. Behind and above her stood a rattled-looking Allegra.

"Ada's sick," said Allegra. "Horrible. Fever." And with that she ran past Anna and down the stairs to throw her arms tightly around Mary.

"I've seen it before, in the convent," Allegra sobbed. "They die. They always die. What if she dies?"

Mary swallowed the news and rocked a little on her feet both from the shock of it and from the sheer force of Allegra's sadness. She shot a look at Jane, who stood dripping in the doorway with her hands to her face.

"Let me see her," said Mary with a confidence she did not possess.

"The doctor is with her now," said Anna.

Just then a shadow fell upon the girls, and it seemed that the air itself had turned to dust. The fine hairs on the nape of Mary's neck stood on end, and her fingertips prickled with dread.

At the top of the stairs was a man of modest height, with fine features and a single, dark eyebrow that seemed tangled in the curls of his hair. His expression was gloomy, and even to look upon him made the girls at the bottom of the stairs tired, so terribly tired.

Despite her sudden onset of weakness, Mary studied the gentleman for any sign of news. He had an otherworldly stare that seemed to look past and through her at the same time.

"Doctor?" asked Jane with anticipation.

The doctor cleared his throat as though he hadn't spoken in a hundred years. His accent was difficult to place—European, but farther afield than France or even Germany—and he spoke slowly.

"Her condition is concerning."

"Pardon me, doctor, but what *is* Lady Ada's condition? What would you have us do?" Mary asked.

He said nothing but remained motionless as the air about him became colder. The man himself was a slow-moving horror, as out of place as a spider on a pillowcase.

"Oh, for heaven's sake," said Jane, balling her hands into fists. "Doctor! The Lady Ada! Is she going to be all right?"

"Fever," said the doctor at last. "I do not like it, no, not one bit."

He descended the stairs in a manner that made it seem as if his upper half were not moving, as though he floated his way down toward the girls.

"Poor thing," the doctor continued. "Poor, poor little thing. Leeches, of course. Yes, leeches . . ."

The girls stood and watched the strange man make it all the way down to the foyer, at which point they pulled themselves away. Finally, the door closed behind the doctor, although none of them had said goodbye.

"I'm going up," said Mary, taking Allegra's shoulders.

Anna collected herself. "I'll put the kettle on," she said as she trotted to the upstairs kitchen.

The door, having been clicked shut for less than ten seconds, burst open without so much as a knock. Mr. Franklin took a step back toward the door as a woman dressed entirely in somber brown, bonnet and all, barged through.

"Where is she?" the intruder asked Mr. Franklin. He paused for a heartbeat and tilted his head ever so slightly up the stairs. Without so much as an "excuse me," she bolted past Jane, Mary, and Allegra.

"And who might you be?" asked Jane, frustration pushing her past the point of courtesy. For all her desire to be a person of Society, it took almost nothing for the feisty, impatient twelve-year-old girl in Jane to surface.

"I should ask the same of you lot," answered the woman without looking back. Mary could not help but notice the stranger's dress was a near match to the matronly, somber brown of Mrs. Somerville's. The three girls looked at one another, shrugged, and followed.

Before they reached the top of the stairs, they heard the door to Ada's room close firmly. Clearly, they were unwelcome.

"Who is she?" asked Allegra.

"I'm not sure, but Mr. Franklin admitted her, so she can't be a total stranger." Mary looked at Allegra. "Tell me what happened."

Allegra's lip was still trembling, her cheeks wet from tears. "Ada went to Lizzie's, for dinner and to stay over," said Allegra. Mary nodded. She knew that bit. "I went to bed, and in the middle of the night a carriage showed up, and there was a coachman pounding on the door, and Mr. Franklin carried Ada inside soaking wet, and Anna sent for the doctor." She began crying again.

"All right, all right," said Mary. "Shush now. I'll look in on Ada and introduce myself to this mystery woman. Let's keep our wits about us, shall we?"

Jane and Allegra nodded in agreement, and Jane took Allegra's small hand. Mary squeezed out the best smile she could and opened the door.

Ada was asleep but shivering. Her skin was yellow-white and rubbery, her lips almost grey. The sight put a fist-sized lump in Mary's stomach. With her back to Mary, the mysterious visitor in brown, still in her cape and bonnet, wrung a cloth in a basin of water and washed Ada's forehead.

"Excuse me," said Mary. "We're all at wits' end with worry. My name is Mary Godwin, and I am a friend of Lady Ada's. I'm pleased to meet you, I'm sure."

"I'm sorry, Miss Godwin," said the woman, "but Lady Ada is in no condition for visitors today, besides which it is news to me that the young lady has any friends whatsoever."

"But I *am* her friend. Her best friend. We study together, under Peebs—that is to say, Mr. Shelley. And we—" Mary stopped herself from saying "And we solve mysteries under the name Wollstonecraft Detective Agency" because while half of London might know the secret, there was no need to inform the other half. "And I'm sorry if I missed your name, Mrs. . . ."

"Woolcott. I am Mrs. Woolcott. And I'm afraid, Miss Godwin, I'm going to have to ask you and your friends to leave at once. If you have any sense at all, you can see that Ada is terribly ill, and this is no place for the chattering of girls."

"They are not my friends, Mrs. Woolcott. One is my sister, and the other is sister to Lady Ada. And she lives here."

Mrs. Woolcott stopped at this and looked at Mary.

"Allegra?" she said in astonishment. "That was Allegra?"

"It was. Rather, she is," asserted Mary.

"The poor thing must be frightened half to death."

"She is, Mrs. Woolcott. We all are."

"I'll see to her briefly, if you don't mind staying with Lady Ada for a moment."

"Not at all," said Mary, relieved to find Mrs. Woolcott proving to be an ally.

Mrs. Woolcott bent to brush the hair from sleeping Ada's forehead, and untied her bonnet, leaving it on the chair. She tiptoed expertly around the piles of drawings, books, tools, and random machine parts scattered on Ada's floor.

Mary took Mrs. Woolcott's place at Ada's side.

Ada had never seemed more doll-like and small, and Mary realized how much of Ada's presence was the sheer force of her mind and personality, which filled every room. But now there was just this poor, sick child, tiny in the vast Marylebone house.

On the side table where Ada usually kept a candle for the night was a space where no candle was, because Ada had not meant to spend the night there. Instead of the candle, there was a scrap of paper. Mary picked it up.

A note, in Ada's handwriting, in pencil. Capital letters. At first it seemed to Mary to be gibberish, nonsense, as the letters didn't spell anything she could pronounce. But then she remembered the *M*'s and *C*'s and *X*'s. Roman numerals. They must mean something. Something important enough to send her into last night's storm and the jaws of this beastly fever.

Mrs. Woolcott returned, and not knowing why, Mary discreetly palmed Ada's note, hiding it from view.

"She doesn't remember me, of course, the dear," said Mrs. Woolcott. "But Allegra was only a baby when last we met. She's grown into quite a fierce little thing."

"Like her sister," said Mary. But Ada didn't seem quite so fierce at the moment. She coughed a little bit in her sleep, her shoulders jerking uncomfortably toward the ceiling. Mrs. Woolcott came to Ada's side, expecting Mary to move out of the way, which she did.

"Do you . . . Can I get you anything?" asked Mary.

"Oh, Miss Cumberland's seen to that, thank you, Miss Godwin," said Mrs. Woolcott, who seemed to know her way about the house as though she belonged there.

"Well, if you'll excuse me then," said Mary, closing Ada's door behind her. She set out for Allegra and Jane, whom she found in the drawing room with a newly arrived Peebs.

He stood up. "Miss Mary, how is she?" he asked.

"I cannot say, or at least I dare not," Mary answered, on the verge of tears. "Dear Allegra, please do tell me more of our Ada's arrival."

"I told you. A coach in the night, and they brought her in just like that."

"That's rather inhospitable," noted Peebs. "Perhaps they thought she would do best under the supervision of her own doctor?"

"But to send her out on an hour's carriage ride—in

that ghastly storm?" accused Jane. "And this Mrs. Woolcott? Who is she? She acted like she knew both Lady Ada and Allegra quite well, although Allegra doesn't remember her." Allegra nodded.

"And she knows Miss Cumberland," Mary added. "I believe she does. I don't know who she is, but she seems to be on our side, or at least on Ada's side, and that will have to do for now." Mary handed Peebs the scrap of paper.

"What do you make of this?"

"Roman numerals," Peebs answered right away. "1780, 1792. This next line is 1808. And 1810 here. More here, here. Why do you ask?"

"I found this on Ada's bedside. It's her handwriting, though the paper is soaked through. She obviously had it with her in the rain. I think it means something."

"I'll wager it does," said Peebs. "This is odd, though. Look—these here and here aren't Roman numerals at all. They're Greek letters. And she's gone over some of these others a few times; she's underlined them—well, underdotted them. Look."

"A code! It must be! Hidden to look like dates. Hardly anyone would notice," said Mary.

"Exactly, real dates, only with something else scattered among them."

"A code meant to look like not-a-code," Mary said slowly, searching for the word.

"Oh!" cried Allegra. "Like in Ada's wizard book!"

"Spies," said Jane cryptically.

"Steganography," said Peebs.

"Peebs," said Mary, "we must send word to Dedlock Hall. To Lizzie. She can tell us what happened, and she'll be able to tell us what this means, surely."

"I shall see to it," said Jane crisply. "A proper letter, at once."

Nodding, Peebs offered his arm to Mary, and they walked to the drawing room.

CONFIDENCES

14

This was not how Mary had imagined the Woll-stonecraft Detective Agency would be. Nothing made sense. *Ada was not supposed to fall ill like this,* she thought. *We should have caught a fishmonger by now.* Alas, there seemed no fishmonger to catch; just a sneaking suspicion of fishiness, a ghost girl who looked rather a lot like a real girl about to marry said fishiness, and a scrap of paper with a maybe-code.

She looked up and found Peebs staring out the window, suddenly looking about a hundred years old.

"Are you all right?" Mary asked.

"Mmm? Yes, I suppose. Although to be fair to circumstance, I seem to have proven myself to be somewhat less than all right."

"However so?"

"It was ever my intention to keep my eye on young Ada. I encouraged this adventure, this Detective Agency—"

"But we kept it a secret from you! It's hardly your fault."

"Come now, Mary. I should hope you hold me in higher esteem than one who would be so easily deceived. I knew. I had hoped to coax Ada out of her shell, as you have done most admirably. But now it seems she has ventured too far, too far out indeed. Off investigating, home after midnight, soaked through. I feel as though I sent her into that storm myself."

"You cannot blame yourself. I should have been with her."

"No, Mary, you should not. Lady Ada is your friend, not your responsibility. Whereas she is mine, and I have failed her."

"You have not failed her yet. Peebs, please hold out a hope. I fear I do not have the strength to bear this hope alone."

"Then we as her friends shall bear this hope to-gether. I do, Mary. I do hope."

Mary smiled a little at this.

"You know," added Peebs, "I have often had the misfortune of being on the wrong side of our Ada. She is an extraordinary creature, and rather formidable."

"And so?"

"Well, I cannot imagine this fever is going to enjoy being in Ada's bad books much either."

Worried as she was, Mary almost laughed at that. She took a deep breath.

"You're a spy," said Mary.

"Yes, we covered that in the middle of your last case."

"You're in a book," Mary pressed.

"Well, yes, I have a few poems published—"

"In Jane's book. On . . . Society."

"Oh, that."

"That."

"Merely an accident of birth. I was born to my father and he to his."

"The first Earl of Castle Goring," said Mary.

"It's not that grand. Or even a castle, really. Castle

Boring, we called it growing up." Peebs chuckled a little.

"So you're rich, to put matters precisely."

Peebs cleared his throat. "My family has means. I on the other hand have a modest allowance. I have little interest in my family's fortunes, as my destiny is poetry, not wealth. As for being a spy, yes, I placed myself in the Byron household to keep my eye on Ada, as I promised her father. Knowing her mother would not approve, I had to remain . . ."

"Clandestine."

"Clandestine, as you say."

"But you're not just a spy in Ada's house," she said. "You're a spy in mine as well."

"Ah," said Peebs.

"Ah, indeed," said Mary accusingly. "You're my father's patron. You give him money. That's how we live. Because of you."

"Not at all. Your father and your stepmother are both esteemed publishers who—"

"Who couldn't rub tuppence ha'penny together if they roasted chestnuts, yes, I know. We clearly need your money. I just don't know why you would choose to keep such matters from me."

"I assure you I was not being clandestine, merely discreet. And I am certain your father would not appreciate the discussion of such matters with his fourteen-year-old daughter. I'm afraid, Mary, that we are to leave it at that."

"But—"

"At that," said Peebs with finality.

Mary crossed her arms. She had recently learned something about herself—she resented not knowing something the minute a question occurred to her. *I really am turning into Ada,* she thought.

CHURCH RECORDS

15

Ada woke often in the night, muttering with delirium, like a swimmer coming up for breath. Each time, a sleepless Mrs. Woolcott would cheer her on, wipe her brow with a cool cloth, and offer a sip of water.

In Somers Town, Mary was equally restless, dreaming of Roman numerals, which swam about in an ocean of her own head, waves pooling in the little dots drawn beneath the odd letter here and there. She woke with Jane's cold knees pressed against her back and waited for dawn, making pictures on the ceiling with her imagination.

Her brother's cries were almost a relief—at last she could rise and turn her ideas into actions.

Fires, kettle, breakfast, and baby attended to. Basin and dressing and chores, cape and bonnet and Jane's chatter, and finally the grey of Polygon Road and a black carriage and a reading boy who pretended he wasn't there. Jane debarked from the carriage at Marylebone with a serious nod to her sister, but Mary remained inside with Charles.

As usual, some fiddling was required to allow Charles a day off from his job at the boot-polish factory, and Mary waited safely inside the carriage while this mysterious business was conducted. But at last Charles emerged, and they made their way west.

Church records. It had come to Mary in the night. They had dates, but what did they mean? They must relate to the Earnshaw family, or Ada wouldn't have thought them important. She would have liked to ask Lizzie, but they'd had no response to the letter they'd sent her the day before, which was worrisome. *What would a detective do next?* Mary wondered, trying hard to feel like one. And then it came to her: a church near Dedlock Hall must have the birth, marriage, and death records for the whole family, going back forever. They had the years—they just needed to find what had happened in them.

Kensington was a new direction for Charles, and it was the most expensive carriage ride of his life. He was grateful for the shillings Mary had brought along, folded in a sheet of paper that never left her gloved hand.

They exited the carriage at a compact and bustling market, flanked by churches. Mary took mental notes of everything, trying to get her bearings. To the north lay Shepherd's Bush, and the river was to their south, though she couldn't catch its familiar stink.

They wandered the market in the guise of brother and sister, weaving among carts and stalls and ignoring wary-eyed merchants who glanced at Charles's clothes and watched his hands. They had just decided in which church to begin their investigation when Charles sensed a movement in a narrow alley between two brick buildings as they passed.

Experience had taught Charles not to look too closely. He sidled closer to Mary and picked up his steps.

"Find the will" came a voice behind them. They turned.

The ghost. Charles knew at once this was Mary's girl in grey, the one he had hunted in Regent's Park. Frenzied look, grey gown, auburn hair, she could be no other.

"You! Are you all right?" Mary's words tumbled out before she could think. "Good heavens, but you're the spitting image of—"

"You were watching me in Regent's Park," Charles interrupted.

She nodded. "You have to help me, you have to save Lizzie. I heard them talking."

"Lizzie?" asked Mary. "But how? Heard who talking?"

"Find the will. The will is the key. It locks him out." Her eyes darted about the street as though she were afraid of being followed. "Lizzie is in terrible danger. Lock him out!" With that she dashed into the street, where the throng of people and carts and horses and barrels made it easy for her to disappear. Charles thought to chase her, but she had vanished.

"All right, Miss Mary?" Charles asked, hoping he sounded less rattled than he felt.

"Well, better for having my senses restored to trustworthiness. That girl was no ghost. But the resemblance . . . What does she mean, 'Lizzie is in danger'? Oh! Charles! She knows Lizzie—so the two cases *are* related. But how?"

"She said something about a will, and that means dying, miss," said Charles. "And that means church records. So it would seem the task before us is unchanged."

"Quite right, Master Dickens. Church records. Onward."

The verger at the first church was kind enough to direct Mary and Charles to the second, where records for all parish activities were kept. Weddings and christenings and funerals, the locations of graves, and records too of church holdings; farms and orphanages, docks and estates left by those with no one else to leave things to. "All going back to the last fire," the verger had said, and this was some eighty years ago.

This was no *Times* archive, with neatly folded grey blankets of words, tidily stacked and neatly labeled.

This was an Ada's-bedroom-floor of sliding piles of notebooks, mostly cheaply clothbound and dog-eared things from the previous century. And none of it printed either, but penned in flecking brown ink, writ small to save space, line to line.

Charles looked at Mary and raised an eyebrow.

"We need to make a plan," she said. "We have dates ranging from 1780 to 1812 on the list. I'll work forward from 1780 and you work backward from 1812, and we'll meet in the middle."

"Any idea where 1812 would be?" asked Charles.

"Not yet. If you take this corner here, I'll start over there. Take a ledger top and bottom of a stack and read the dates. I'll do the same, and we'll see if there's a pattern. If not, we'll each take a step closer to the center and see what dates those ledgers reveal. We should at least see if we're getting warmer."

Charles nodded, and Mary crossed the room, thinking Ada would be proud of her for being so methodical.

Charles opened the first slim book on the top of his pile. "Farm receipts, 1782. I say, that doesn't seem much for a pig." He pulled a ledger from the bottom of the pile. "1782 as well."

Mary picked up the hem of her skirt with one hand while undoing the string on her bonnet with the other. She placed the bonnet on a stack that seemed slightly less dusty than the others.

"1769," she said, looking at the first date that was (conveniently) written on the cover of the first ledger she saw. She took another from the stack. "1770." She looked at Charles, and they each took a large step to the right and tried new piles.

"1810," said Charles.

"1779," said Mary, smiling.

Each took another side step, and they were there.

"1812," Charles said.

"1780!" said Mary, with excitement.

"Shall we go through that pile together?" Charles asked.

"No, I'll excavate down and go backward in time. You go through that one and see if we can't sneak up on it."

"And, er, what are we looking for?"

"Dedlock Hall, anything involving the Earnshaws or Dedlock Hall. Although . . ."

"Yes?" asked Charles.

"I just had a dreadful thought. What we're looking

135

for—it's likely a secret. Or perhaps several secrets. That wouldn't be here, would it? I mean to say, everything in these notebooks is something witnessed, something legal. Not secret at all." She was disheartened at this realization.

"No such thing as a secret, Miss Mary," Charles explained. "There's always a trace somewhere, and I reckon here's the place. It all ends up here, names and dates and the whole works. Nobody comes looking—that's the only thing makes it secret."

Mary sighed, the heartbreak of it all tugging at the hem of her attention. She shook it off.

"Dedlock then," she said, attending to the matter at hand. But Charles was already somewhere in the spring of 1812.

STORYBOOK PAGES

16

"Twins!" said Mary, staring at the baptism certificate in the lurching carriage. In her ungloved hands was a sheaf of paper, each sheet a hasty copy of a document found in the church records office. Across from her, bouncing at every pothole, sat Charles with a similar bundle.

"Elizabeth and Alice, born to Calpurnia and George Earnshaw, 1810. So . . . Lizzie has a sister? Is this our ghost girl?"

"It would seem so, Miss Mary."

"But then look at this," said Mary, presenting

another note. "The two girls were accepted by the church for adoption, to be placed with another family. Lizzie's adoption is here, but I couldn't find one for Alice.

"But why?" asked Mary. "What would make a couple surrender their own children?"

"Poverty? I've known families so poor, they placed a child for adoption just to know she would be fed."

"That's horrid," said Mary, her heart breaking at the thought.

"It is," agreed Charles.

"It's also a conundrum."

"What's a conundrum?"

"It means a difficult puzzle," said Mary.

"Thank you, Miss Godwin, for that most edifying definition." Charles smirked.

Mary looked up and smiled. "Oh—sorry, of course. I meant I don't understand why we have a record of Lizzie's adoption when we know she lived with her father until he died."

"Well . . ." Charles shuffled through his documents. "Yes, here's a note showing the Earnshaws adopting a baby in 1813. And here, I found their marriage certificate. It matches one of the dates on the list," said Charles.

"Oh, I copied their marriage as well. Silly of me."

"Did you? I didn't see you at that ledger," noted Charles with some curiosity.

"Yes, it's right here, look," said Mary, flipping pages. Charles did the same, and they exchanged their papers.

"Our copies are different—one must be wrong." She handed Charles's copy back to him.

"This baffles me, I must admit," said Charles. "No, look, same people, different dates. Two weddings."

"Two weddings? Why would the same people get married twice?"

"Well, the earlier one, here, was officiated by the parson and witnessed by the verger," said Charles. "People who work in the church, likely to be there any day. But here's my copy . . ."

"Two years later," finished Mary. "Signed by the bishop himself, and witnessed by Lord and Lady Illegible. What do you make of it, Charles?" Mary asked.

"Well, the first has the feel of a paupers' wedding.

No family. Just a 'Will you marry us please and be quick about it.' "

"A secret wedding!" exclaimed Mary. "And the second?"

"A society wedding, by the looks of it," said Charles. "Still, as you say, a conundrum."

Mary looked out the window. For all their research, they were no closer to making sense of it all.

"We need to give this some sort of shape," she mused.

"Yes?"

Again Mary paused. They were still ages from home.

"Once upon a time," murmured Mary.

"I beg your pardon?"

"Dates. People . . . Let's play a game. Or rather, let's tell a story. Look, let's place all our papers in order by date, and we'll make a little story out of it as we go along."

Charles agreed. "All right. I believe I have our beginning."

"Once upon a time . . . ," said Mary, leading.

"Once upon a time, a young lady was born to a

wealthy West London family and baptized by the bishop, with a Lady Smoodge here as godmother."

"Smoodge?" asked Mary.

"With your forgiveness, I'm afraid I was unable to make out the signature."

Mary nodded. "And so the little girl grew up in a great house. And one day, she fell in love with a fellow named George and was married at the little church there in the market square."

"But a very poor wedding," continued Charles. "Not the wedding one would expect for a girl growing up in a grand house."

"Because . . . *George* was poor," Mary surmised. "And they eloped, out of love. A secret wedding! How utterly romantic."

"And here," said Charles, shuffling papers and handing over a note, "is an acknowledgment of rents paid on a church-owned farm."

"So he just worked a church farm?"

"It would seem so," said Charles.

"And then—such joy. Two baby girls, born to a couple in love," Mary romanticized. "It was the best of times."

"It was the worst of times," said Charles grimly,

presenting notes showing mounting debts on the farm and, finally, the note showing that the couple had placed the children with the church for adoption.

"But I don't understand. Why would Calpurnia's family turn their backs on her? And her daughters?"

"Scandal, Miss Mary, or the threat of it. She married a pauper, clearly without her family's permission, and chose a pauper's lot. But there is a turn, here, in our story," said Charles. "A year later, here is a donation to the church, and a handsome one at that, from George Earnshaw."

"Four hundred pounds a year!" cried Mary, reading the slip of paper. "From holdings in . . . Jamaica?"

"It would seem that the young Mister Earnshaw, having been driven to desperation by poverty, traveled abroad to seek his fortune. And made it, in an extraordinary amount of time."

"Good heavens" was all Mary could say.

"And here is the second wedding certificate. The bishop and lords and ladies attending."

"A proper Society wedding, as Jane would say."

"It would seem so," said Charles. "Her pauper a prince at last, he now presents himself as a suitable suitor, and they can be married publicly, their past behind them."

"But they must find their lost children," said Mary, adding another page to the story. "And at last they find, and adopt, Lizzie, their own daughter, and return to Dedlock Hall in happiness, as a family."

"But no sign of Alice," said Charles. "And another sad turn here. Lizzie's mother passes away, of fever, to be buried on the grounds of Dedlock Hall in a new mausoleum." Charles held the papers documenting the blessing of the crypt and the burial of Lizzie's mother, but all Mary could think of in that instant was the word "fever." Worry for Ada was the weight of a hundred books on her chest. She rallied herself and returned to the story.

"So Lizzie and her father comfort each other, and make a life together, rattling about that huge estate, with Lizzie apparently never learning of Alice."

"And there the story seems to end," said Charles, disappointed.

"I can't imagine that Mr. Earnshaw would ever stop looking for his lost girl. . . . How sad that we should find her instead." Suddenly Mary sat up straight. "Oh!"

"Miss Mary?"

"Maybe he *did* find her. Maybe that was the good news he wrote to Mrs. Somerville about!"

"But . . . how did Alice come to be running in front of our carriage? When did she become an escaped lunatic?"

Mary slumped in her seat again. "I have no idea."

LEECHES

17

Later that afternoon, burdened with story and sneezy with dust, Mary and Charles entered the Marylebone house. Allegra was on her way up the stairs as Miss Cumberland was on her way down, and at the top loomed the eerie dark-browed doctor. Peebs stood immediately behind Mary.

"Leeches!" said Allegra. "There were leeches."

"Best thing for fever," said the doctor in his strange accent. "Leeches."

"Horrible squirmy black things," added Allegra.

She noted something disturbingly leech-like in the doctor himself.

"Is Ada awake?" Mary asked.

"A little," answered Allegra. "She's not making any sense. She sort of mumbles and falls asleep again. But she's asking for you."

"Can I see her?"

Miss Cumberland nodded, trotting down the stairs to what must have been her hundredth kettle boiling of the day.

"John?" asked Peebs of the doctor, who gave a slow, resigned shrug, as though to slough off the dread that clung to him like a fog.

"The worst is over, I suspect," the doctor said. "But the child is very weak."

The grim fellow let himself out without a further word, leaving only the echo of a chill in his wake.

"You know him?" asked Allegra.

"Doctor Polidori was a friend and traveling companion of your father's—one of the few the baroness has yet to exile, evidently," said Peebs. "Now, why don't you tell me about the leeches?" And he led her off to the library, out of everyone's way. Charles followed Peebs, as it seemed the only appropriate thing to do.

Mary wondered where Jane had gotten to.

As soon as Mary entered Ada's room, she felt that something was terribly wrong. Before her was something she'd never seen before: Ada's floor.

Gone were the mushrooming mounds of drawings and plans, the hunks of machine parts and disassembled gears, stray rusty tools, and upturned inkpots. Instead there was just . . . floor.

Mary looked past the still-sleeping Ada in the bed to Mrs. Woolcott, beside her.

"What have you done?" Mary asked.

"I've just tidied up a bit, dear, not to worry."

"What have you done?"

"Well, you can't have thought it was like that all the time, can you?" answered Mrs. Woolcott. "Ordinarily I'd smooth out her papers and run them to the attic, and she'd take them to the balloon. But I see you've done away with that. She must miss it terribly."

"She does, and who *are* you?" Mary asked rudely.

"Miss Godwin, I do realize the circumstances are extraordinary, but there is simply no cause for such an accusatory tone. I was not the one who led to the destruction of Lady Ada's balloon—"

"No, who are you, really?" Mary was quite beside herself.

At this, Ada stirred. Mary rushed to her bedside, and Mrs. Woolcott picked up a glass of water.

Ada's eyes fluttered, and opened slightly. They reminded Mary of glass marbles.

"Miss Coverlet?" croaked Ada, her lips parched from fever.

"Here. You hush now, Ada. Don't try to speak. You're a bit woozy from the leeches, so best rest up now."

Ada looked slowly around the room.

"Mary?" she said.

Mary realized she was squeezing Ada's hand very tightly, and that she was crying.

"I'm here. Oh, Ada, I'm so glad you're awake. There's so much to tell you—"

"A secret wife," mumbled Ada weakly as she was drifting off. "Find the ghost. Find . . . the will."

The mention of a will shot a chill through Mary—echoes of the words of the ghost girl. There was a knock on the open door.

"Mary?" said Jane, the great grey newspaper in

her hand. "You'll wish to see this." Mrs. Woolcott shot Jane an icy look.

"Not now, Jane," said Mary in a hush. But Ada was already asleep, grey and raspy.

"No, honestly, now. It's the afternoon paper, and it just arrived. Look."

Jane crossed the too-empty floor like a ship with a large grey sail in front. "Here," she said, shaking one hand to show Mary the page. The words were tall and narrow: ESCAPED LUNATIC APPREHENDED.

"It's your ghost," said Jane. "At the hospital, part of the College of Physicians in—"

"Regent's Park," Mary finished.

Mary's mind raced. How could Alice be apprehended and the story in the newspaper already? She'd seen her just this morning!

"Enough, girls," scolded Mrs. Woolcott. "Lady Ada needs rest, not a newspaper. Now out, the pair of you!" Mrs. Woolcott gathered linens and headed off to fetch more, attempting to herd both Jane and Mary out of the room.

"I beg your pardon," said Jane, exasperated, "and I do realize we keep asking this of you, but who are you, exactly, that you know such things?"

Mrs. Woolcott looked as though she were about to be cross with Jane but then shrugged slightly. "You know who I am. But I think you mean to ask who I was, which is to say Miss Coverlet, Lady Ada's nurse and governess since she was a baby—and, I suspect, since I was scarcely older than yourself, Miss Mary."

At this bit of information the floor of Mary's brain became slightly less cluttered and, she dared to think, slightly less hazardous. It was about time something started making sense.

"Miss Coverlet," Mary said. "You left to marry, and therefore you left service, and this very household, now to return as Mrs. Woolcott."

"As you say, Miss Mary. Now may I attend to these linens?"

Mary nodded and realized that she still clutched the jumble of notes from her expedition in her chilled hand, among them Ada's list that was both Roman numerals and not, because of the Greek.

She took the scrap of paper and laid it on the desk, flattening it out as best she could, and slid it back beside a polished brass lamp, seeing her own fingers upside down and distorted in the metal's reflection.

But so too was the message on the paper. The Greek letters, the larger of the Roman numerals. Upside down in the reflection, it almost looked like—

"Mary?" Ada murmured, waking. "I'm hungry."

JAM BUTTY

A pale and blanket-swaddled Ada descended the stairs, and a once-hushed household erupted.

"Ada! You are not to be out of bed in your state!" said a disapproving Mrs. Woolcott.

"Ada!" cried Mary, whirling around. "I was fetching something for you. You needn't have gotten up!"

"Ada! You're awake!" cried Jane.

"And a relief to see you so, Miss Ada." Peebs smiled.

"Good day to you, Miss Ada," added Charles.

"You look terrible," said Allegra.

"I want to know what's going on," said Ada thinly,

giving a weak effort at a stomp on the stair. "And a jam butty."

If possible, Mrs. Woolcott's disapproval deepened, but she gave a resigned sigh. "You may have a *brief* conversation with your visitors and something to eat while sitting tucked up by the fire in the library. Then it's back to bed with you."

Everyone rushed to make a comfortable place for Ada, and Allegra, having adopted Ada's penchant for bread and butter, fetched just what she wanted from the upstairs kitchen and handed Ada some of that morning's bread with a dollop of butter and jam on a small white plate. Ada nodded appreciatively and tucked in.

When she had finished, Ada raised a finger. "Where are we." It was not a question.

"Church records," Mary said.

"What are those?" Allegra asked.

"Well, it's a list," explained Mary. "A very, very long list, about who married whom and when, and when babies were born, and then who died and was buried. Orphanages and adoptions too. All these events, all these dates, draw a kind of picture. Births, marriages, relations . . . a family tree."

"Aha!" cried Jane, presenting her well-loved copy

of *Burke's Peerage, Baronetage, and Knightage*. She opened a page at random to a well-known Society family. "Like this," she continued, showing Allegra, "but for normal people."

"Exactly," Mary said. "Or in this case, rather extraordinary people, or rather, ordinary people in extraordinary circumstance."

And so Charles and Mary repeated the story of love, and loss, and partial reunion of the Earnshaw family.

"A secret twin," marveled Allegra. "Lizzie will be so happy."

"Except when she finds out her sister is an escaped lunatic," said Jane waspishly. "Oh—recently recaptured lunatic."

"She didn't seem a lunatic when we saw her this morning," offered Mary.

"More scared than mad, I'd say," volunteered Charles.

"I'd be scared if I were married to Sir Caleb too," muttered Ada.

"Married?" asked a shocked Mary.

"He was after the fortune, Alice and Lizzie's fortune," said Ada. "We heard them, Lizzie and I did.

Caleb married Alice, but Lizzie's father figured out that Caleb was a rotter and made sure he was on the outs forever by putting that in his will. Caleb and Bouillabaisse got hold of the will and destroyed it, but there's a copy somewhere, and they're afraid of it. So they got rid of Alice and decided to try again with her sister, the sister who didn't know she was one."

"That's beastly!" cried Mary.

"Mmm," agreed Ada.

"But he's a baronet!" objected Jane.

"So," said Charles, trying to weave this new piece into their story, "Alice gets locked up in the hospital of the College of Physicians, escapes somehow, almost gets run over by our carriage, and is running around London like a ghost."

"And getting apprehended again," added Jane. "It was in the newspaper, just now."

"Good heavens," said Mary. "Alice was warning us that Lizzie was in danger this morning. But she's clearly in danger herself. We must try to rescue her."

Charles was about to speak again when Mrs. Woolcott entered the library.

"Please excuse me," she began, "but Miss Ada needs to rest."

"But—" started Allegra.

"But nothing, dear. It seems I must set the house to rights, as you know I ought. Now off with you, and I'll have Mrs. Chowser make some soup for Lady Ada, and you'll dine in the dining room as in a proper house. In the meantime, off!"

"Quite right," agreed Peebs. "I'll gather my things and be off."

Chastised, although cheerfully, they stood and bowed a little and scuttled out of the library.

In the hall, on the way to Ada's bedroom, Mary pulled them all aside. "We have to get in to see Alice," said Mary.

"I'm coming," insisted Ada.

"You are hardly in any condition—" Mary began.

"Coming," said Ada, resolute.

"We must speak to Lizzie as well, somehow, and warn her of the danger," said Mary.

"We wrote yesterday but we never heard back," said Jane.

"Perhaps Sir Caleb is intercepting her letters?" worried Mary.

"Can we get word to Mrs. Somerville?" asked Charles.

"She was sent off on a ruse," said Ada. "Scotland."

"What's a ruse?" asked Allegra, imagining it as some kind of exotic animal.

"A ploy," explained Mary quietly, which didn't help.

"A wild goose chase," offered Charles, which did.

"We'll have to go to Lizzie ourselves, then. Sneak in tonight," said Jane.

"Sneak where?" asked Peebs from the top of the stairs, giving them all a fright.

"We must get word to Lizzie and warn her," said Mary, "but with Sir Caleb and that evil man about, we have little hope of approaching her directly."

"So you propose to creep out and get a carriage in the middle of the night, to sneak into a young lady's home because you fear she's in danger?" asked Peebs.

"Well . . . yes," said Mary.

"Well, I can hardly allow that," said Peebs. "If she is in danger, then surely you would be in the same danger should you find yourself on the estate again. And you, Lady Ada, not an hour arisen from your sickbed. Therefore I must forbid it."

"Forbid it? You are not my father!" said Mary angrily.

"No, but I am his friend, and your tutor, and the only adult in this fiasco. I cannot permit you to endanger yourself. I shall convey a message myself, and leave at once if you like."

"That's no good at all," said Mary. "Sir Caleb won't let you see her, and I doubt he'll pass on a message."

"Nevertheless, I will try," said Peebs finally. "And you will stay here."

Mary felt like a boiling pot with the lid on. She rattled around her own edges until she met Ada's eyes. Ada gave her a secret half smile, and a secret half nod, and Mary half nodded back as the pot cooled somewhat.

THE HOSPITAL

19

Mrs. Woolcott had taken a brief respite from Ada's bedside to attend to her home and husband, and so Mary had taken the opportunity to see that Ada was as presentable as possible, her hair brushed, wearing her best cape and bonnet, and then Mary, Allegra, and Ada sneaked out the upstairs kitchen door.

Peebs had gone off with a letter for Lizzie. Charles had returned to his family, and even Jane had been persuaded to go home. But Allegra had stuck to Ada's side like a bur, sensing correctly that detecting was about to be done.

It was a short enough walk to Regent's Park from the Marylebone house, even for a weakened Ada, close enough to home for three young girls to stroll unescorted, and along the park path, to the College of Physicians.

Somewhere behind the green-painted door and tall white stone wall was the ghost girl, Alice.

There was no bell rope or knocker. The girls looked about, and there was no one to open the door for them. Shrugging, they pulled the heavy metal handle, and the door groaned open.

The place was silent as a library and sounded hollow. It had the air of learned gentlemen: wet tweed and musty tobacco, old books and the sickly sweet aroma of beard oils and pomades.

They took tentative steps down the echoey hall. A door opened with a start, and a young clerk trotted past them as though they themselves were ghosts. He disappeared around a corner.

There was no one at the reception desk, so the girls crept arm in arm in arm through that strange place, following the fleeing figure for no other reason than that the hallway simply led them in that direction.

Again a door opened unexpectedly, and the man popped out, blinked twice at the girls, and offered a dubious "Can I help you?"

Mary wore a well-rehearsed smile. "Yes, thank you kindly, sir. We are here to visit Mrs. Gulpidge."

"Mrs. Gulpidge?"

"Yes, we are . . . cousins of hers, and we have brought her some comforts of home." Mary gave Ada a prod with an elbow, who in turn prodded Allegra, and at this Allegra produced first a dramatic nod and then a small basket covered with a handkerchief.

"Mrs. Gulpidge," the clerk repeated, only this time with a bit less of a question in his tone.

"Mrs. Caleb Gulpidge. We are of the understanding she is a patient here."

"I'm not certain I recall a Mrs.—" he began.

"She's in the hospital," said Allegra cheerfully.

"Oh dear," said the clerk. "I'll have to check with the doctor to see if she is receiving visitors."

"Oh, it's perfectly all right, I'm sure," said Mary. "In fact, we have a note right here from her doctor, saying that a visit from her loving cousins would be the best thing for her. Don't we, Allegra?"

"Umm," said Allegra.

"May I see this note?" the man asked.

"But of course. Allegra, please show this gentleman the note."

"Umm," said Allegra again.

"Oh, you silly poppet-head. Did you leave it at home? I did say it was terribly important and you were not to lose it. Didn't I tell you?" insisted Mary.

"Umm," said Allegra, a third time. Ada coughed.

"I'm afraid," said the clerk, "that without authorization it would be imposs—"

"Oh, you know little girls," said Mary forcefully. "Always thinking about dolls and ribbons and never remembering important things like doctors' notes. The fact remains, sir, that we do possess exactly the authorization we require."

"You possess it, yet it is not in your possession?" he asked, confused.

"Dolls and ribbons," said Allegra, although through gritted teeth.

"Ah, well, that's, um, I see. Well, please follow me, ladies," the man said, relenting.

There was rather a great deal more hallway than

they expected, and more turns and turn-agains than they could keep track of. The air took on a worried, desperate quality, and the hair began to bristle on the backs of their necks. Ada squeezed Mary's arm in hers.

At the end of one long, white-painted hall was a long, white-painted door. Approaching it, their escort seemed to have second thoughts.

"Are you quite certain you have—"

"Thank you, sir, for your assistance in our compliance with her doctor's explicit and direct orders to visit and provide solace to our cousin. It really is most kind of you."

He paused. His bottom lip seemed to go sideways for a moment, as though it were having some sort of argument with his top lip, and the bottom lip was winning.

"I'm sorry—if you young ladies would stay here for a moment, I'll be right back after I check on something. You may remain here or, if you prefer, return on some other occasion." Curtly, he turned on his heel and was about to walk away when Allegra seemed to suddenly lose her balance, knocking into the fellow.

"I say!" he said, startled.

"Tripped. Sorry," said Allegra, giving him her biggest eyes and lashes.

Frowning, the clerk strode back down the hall away from them, clicking as he went.

"Oh bother," sighed Mary. "And it was going so well. Now what do we do?"

Allegra gave Mary a playful push. "Dolls and ribbons!" she said with a grin, then handed Ada a leather loop with a dozen brass keys.

"Allegra! Did you pick his pockets?"

"You grow up in a convent, you learn a thing or two." Allegra shrugged.

Ada began at once to try each key in the white door, while the others kept watch. On the third try, there was a loud click as satisfying as it was terrifying. The girls looked at one another for a full second before opening the door.

As bright as it was, lit through slender windows set high up on the wall, there was a darkness to the place. The white paint had been replaced with grey, and with each step the girls seemed to wade through the still air of sickness. Narrow metal doors lined the corridor, each door leading to a narrow room with a narrow bed. Each cold iron door seemed to cast its own chill into the hallway.

Ada, Allegra, and Mary proceeded in slow motion, arm in arm. Mary could tell with each step that Ada was beginning to flag. Through each door could be heard its own heartbreak—a sob, a muttering, a cough—and each small sound seemed to steal something from their hearts and push a leaden cold into their ribs. They could scarcely stand it.

"It's all right, you know," whispered Mary. "We've done this sort of thing before."

"Prison," agreed Ada. "And my feet didn't work."

"And here you are, you ferocious thing, having fought off a beastly fever, and your feet working perfectly."

"They are a bit heavy," Ada said, frowning.

"That you're out of bed at all is testament to your fortitude."

"I'm just stubborn, I think," admitted Ada.

"You are," agreed Allegra. "Stubborn."

"Well, we have that in our favor." Mary smiled and gave Ada another squeeze of encouragement.

The hallway ended not in a door but a doorway. Beyond was a large, near-empty room, with only a scattering of chairs and a single patient, a girl, seated with her back to them. Mary saw her grey gown and the auburn hair.

"Alice?" asked Ada, stepping forward. The girl turned, her hair catching the thin light. There was a curious distance in her expression, the spark gone out of her eyes, but to Ada she was unmistakable.

"Lizzie!" Ada cried, and ran to her, Mary immediately behind. "Lizzie, how did you get here? Are you all right?"

Lizzie—for indeed it was Lizzie, and not Alice as they had expected—slowly reached out and touched first Ada's face, then Mary's. She moved as though she were in a dream.

"Ada?" Lizzie asked softly.

"What's wrong with her?" asked Allegra.

"Medicine," Mary answered. "They give you medicine in such places, to keep you calm. Oh, Lizzie, we have to get you out of here."

"You'll do no such thing" came a booming voice from the doorway. Instinctively they looked around for another door, or a window—any avenue for escape—but all they saw was a rack of long, pale canes, their purpose all too menacing.

The voice belonged to a round gentleman with protruding grey muttonchops, his suit fine and his waistcoat scarlet. He ended each sentence with a bang of his walking stick on the floor.

"Who are you girls?" *Bang.* "On what pretense do you interfere with my patient?" *Bang.* "How did you get in here?" *Bang.*

"There's been a mistake, doctor." Mary assumed the man was a doctor, given the finery of his clothes and the way he acted as if he owned the place. "This is not Alice Gulpidge but her twin sister, Lizzie."

"I knew you girls were trouble," said the man behind the doctor. "Dolls and ribbons indeed."

Allegra popped out from behind Mary and rudely stuck her tongue out at him.

"I should call the constabulary!" said the doctor, blocking the door with his stick. "In fact, I mean to. You there, alert the constable."

Quick as anything, Allegra moved to the wall and removed a long, whippy cane. She pointed it at the doctor.

"Move your walking stick, doctor. Mary, Ada, take Lizzie and go."

"Impudent child!" shouted the doctor, and aimed

his stick right at Allegra. "Put down that cane at once!"

"You first," said Allegra. With that, the doctor swung his stick to knock her cane out of the way, but she swished it to the side, so that he missed completely, and she returned pointing her cane straight at the doctor's face.

"Wretch!" the doctor exclaimed, again trying to beat the cane from Allegra's hand. She darted it out and parried it like a sword, tapping first one side, then the other. She seemed to be enjoying herself.

"Go!" she said to Mary. Mary gathered Lizzie up, half carrying her, and moved toward the door. Ada could do little but follow. The young man tried to bar their way, but Allegra lunged forward to poke him in the belly with her cane.

"Hey! Gerroff!" he said, trying to pluck the cane from the air. Allegra's cane was too quick. Mary used that moment to push both Lizzie and Ada ahead of her, out the doorway and down the long grey hall—leaving Allegra and the two men to duel in the big room.

The doctor had clearly lost his temper now, and he swung the stick not at Allegra's cane but at the

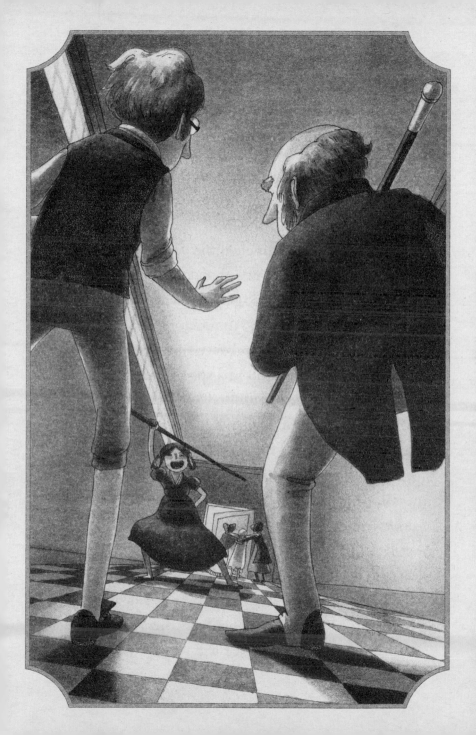

girl herself, who stepped and parried, all in a circle, so that now their situations were reversed: the men in the room, and Allegra in the doorway. She could see behind her that the other girls had made it to the far end of the hallway and opened the locking metal door that separated the asylum from the rest of the college.

While she was distracted, the young man rushed her, but she whacked his ear, nearly losing her cane in the process but allowing her a few vital steps backward. Finally, at wits' end, the doctor thrust his walking stick straight at Allegra's face—but she caught the attack with her cane and in a spiral motion wrapped the force of his thrust around and around, sending his stick spinning out of his hand and behind her down the corridor.

"The disarm!" she said, delighted. "Ada! I did it!"

Glancing backward, Allegra could see Mary at the door, ready to open it further or, she feared, shut it altogether. In one last, desperate move, she poked a wrist and a belly and a nose, then turned to run. The clerk made one last, desperate grab for her, but Allegra twirled out of his reach and then sprinted for the barely open door. Once she was through, Mary clanged it shut and locked it with the key she had at the ready, trapping the angry men behind it.

Allegra looked up at Ada, catching her breath.

"Told you bendy could be useful," she said, and was rewarded with a small smile from Ada.

"That, Miss Byron, was rather terribly impressive," granted Mary. "But we have to get Lizzie out of here, and Ada needs help too."

So Allegra supported Ada, and Mary held up Lizzie, and the four of them took one corner and another, not really caring if they found the door they'd first come through—anything leading out would do—but by some fate managed to find themselves where they had begun. As before, there was no one about, so Mary set the loop of keys on a doorknob and pushed the main door out into the late afternoon of Regent's Park.

Mr. Franklin scarcely raised an eyebrow to find four young ladies in the foyer, one of whom was barely conscious. He simply scooped Lizzie up and inclined his head toward the stairs so that the girls might precede him and show him which room to place her in.

When she was safely ensconced in a guest bed-room, with Ada "I might rest for just a bit" lying next to her, Mary had a moment to wonder:

"If we've got Lizzie, who's got Alice?"

She wasn't expecting an answer, as of course Alice could be anywhere—she could still be wandering the alleys of Kensington where Mary'd last seen her this morning. So Mary was stunned when Lizzie quite clearly said, "They do," before slipping off into sleep.

THE CRYPT

20

It was a dark and stormy night.

The full fury of freezing rain had not returned from the other evening, but the wind had winter on its mind and sought every gap in the folds of Mary's cloak. Lanternless, they were a good ways from Dedlock Hall but had given the coachman strict instructions. He was more than a little reluctant to take them in the first place, guessing their ages, and even less willing to drop three young girls off so far from anywhere on such a ghastly night, but the last of Mary's pocket money was surrendered, and he did as she asked.

Alongside, Ada was bundled in one of her mother's cloaks, better for the weather if a bit too long for the eleven-almost-twelve-year-old, and trawling mud. As much as Mary would have preferred Ada return to bed and recover, she knew there was no denying her friend's nature.

Jane too would not be denied this trip. She'd suspected that Mary was trying to get rid of her earlier, and so she had delivered a message to their parents that *both* sisters would be spending the night at the Byron house, and returned, overnight bag in hand. She wished she'd thought to bring a warmer cloak, or warmer shoes, or warmer anything as the three girls walked in silence, and in worry, through the black night.

They had spent the entire evening trying to talk themselves out of it.

Peebs had sent word that he hadn't succeeded in seeing Lizzie, but that was no surprise—Lizzie was with them. Did Lizzie even know what she was saying, though? Did she really mean that Alice was being held at Dedlock Hall? Did she even know that Alice existed?

But in the end there was nothing for it—if there was a chance Alice was in danger, they had to try to help.

Her frozen fingers keeping her cloak closed, Mary trudged and trod through the mud ruts in the road. She had a box of matches, if it came to that, but feared the light would attract attention. The wind made eerie creaking noises in the branches of roadside trees.

They made good time as the wind sped them on, and within ten minutes or so they saw the trees thin out, and saw too the lights of the great manor house across the green. Off to the left was the stone mausoleum, and it was this that they first wanted to visit. Whatever it was that Ada had suspected, she knew the key was in the Roman numerals, and she wanted another look.

Mary felt the most pressing thing was to find Alice as quickly as possible and get them all back safely to Marylebone. Ada paused, gripping the wet bark of a white tree, catching her breath. Mary feared Ada's fever might return if their mission lasted a moment longer than necessary—perhaps even if they turned back at that moment. Jane held Ada's hands in an effort to warm them and looked up at her big sister for some kind of direction. Mary wished she had some to give.

As they approached the crypt from behind, Mary's

blood ran cold. There was a sound coming from the tomb, where no living sound should be.

Sobbing.

Every ghost story Mary had read or imagined arose fully before her. She thought she should pray, but her mind was a flurry of cave bats, and no prayer would settle in her memory. She swallowed and pressed on.

She dared peek quickly about the corner to the front of the crypt and back again, her heart trying to break its way out of her ribs and run back up the road without her.

"There's no one there," whispered Mary.

"You've seen a ghost before," said Ada. "And it was just a girl. Nothing to be afraid of. Go on."

That makes sense, thought Mary. *If there's a sound inside, it's a girl, not a ghost.* It must be Alice—it had to be Alice. She would be in need of an ally, glad of their company, and grateful for the assistance they were there to deliver. Mary steeled herself, stood up straight, and walked to the iron grille of the tomb.

"Alice?" she asked of the darkness.

There was no answer, only further sobbing, but an exhausted sobbing, the kind that comes from several hours of it with no relief.

"Alice?" Mary tried again, this time daring a match. The match hissed and spat against the wind, but Mary sheltered the dancing flame with her palm and held it between the iron bars to light the tomb. Now there were two lights: the match, and its twin reflected in the tarnished silver mirror set in the ceiling. There on the cold stone floor sat a girl tucked into a ball, crying. Mary was horrified to discover that the girl was wearing only a nightdress in the bitter cold.

"Good heavens," said Mary, quickly opening the latch, swinging up the wrought-iron bar, pushing in the grillework door, and finding a lantern tucked into the corner. She gave more light to the small stone room and saw a basket, a pitcher, and a chamber pot recently left in this makeshift prison. "Oh, Alice, let's get you out of here."

It was indeed Alice, Mary's ghost girl from Regent's Park, who was not all right, not all right at all.

Mary whipped off her cloak and wrapped it around the shivering girl as Ada rushed in to help.

"Who has done this to you?" Ada asked.

"It was Caleb," said Alice, burying her face into Mary's shoulder. "My . . . husband."

"Come now—we'll get you sorted. I must say you sound less . . . distracted."

"It was the medicine. Caleb had the doctors lock me away and give me that vile stuff. But they were careless, and I managed to escape."

"Into Regent's Park," said Mary. "My ghost girl."

"Oh, am I interrupting?" came a menacing voice. Sir Caleb loomed in the crypt's entrance, a horribly smug look on his face. "I saw the light and wondered if we had unwelcome visitors."

"Scoundrel!" spat Mary, livid at what this cruel man had done to poor Alice.

"Scoundrel?" countered Sir Caleb. "I am merely attending to my bride-to-be, in conditions to which she has become accustomed."

"This is how you treat your wife, sir?" said Mary, furious.

"My wife? No, no, Miss Godwin. This is Lizzie, my fiancée. We are to be married at first light, and off to Jamaica with the tide. Then she shall indeed be my wife, and the Earnshaw fortune shall be mine!"

"You cannot switch people!" Ada scoffed.

"But I have, you see! What was Alice is Lizzie, and Lizzie is Alice. The medicine tends to confuse them."

Sir Caleb seemed to have found a coward's brav-
ery now that he had three girls trapped before him.
The gloating man continued. "Your father may have
tried to thwart me, but with him, as you see beneath
you, deceased, he can no longer interfere. I am free to
marry Lizzie here."

"You cannot be married to two people at the same
time," said Mary. "That is against the law!"

"But this girl and I are already married. So what is
the harm? All that stands between me and the Earnshaw fortune is a mere name. Lizzie, Alice, Alice,
Lizzie . . . I shall marry and I shall be on my way to
Jamaica before anyone is the wiser."

"*I* will be wiser," came a voice from the darkness
outside. A cloaked figure approached. A girl's voice,
strong with fury.

Jane.

"How *dare* you exploit this family so! How *dare* you
disgrace the grave of their father with your foul deeds."

Sir Caleb jumped backward into the tomb, knocking the oil lantern over in the process, smashing it
to pieces. A jet of flame the height of a man shot up
to roar in the darkness—trapping the villain and the
girls in the crypt.

"You scoundrel," continued Jane from beyond the flame, a fever spirit incarnate. "You monstrosity. You horrid, horrid man!"

Sir Caleb was still in shock and had not realized that it was Jane beneath the cowl. All he could see were flames, and all he could hear were the words of accusation from which there was no escape, issued from this dark, hooded specter. His judgment at last.

Mary took Alice by the shoulders, so they were face to face. "Alice! Ever jump through a bonfire?"

"At Mayday." Alice nodded.

"Right, then," said Mary. "Ada? Quick as snapdragons. One, two . . . three!" And the three girls darted through the flames, as quick as Mr. Hazzlit's fingers through the dinner-table candle, as quick as plucking plums from brandy fire, emerging quite unharmed on the other side. Alice turned, wheeling Mary's woolen cloak from her shoulders and dropping its weight on the flames, putting them out in a swallow of darkness. There was a screech as she slammed the iron grille into place and snapped it tight with both bar and latch that had moments before imprisoned her.

In the chill dark night, the four girls embraced. Ada swooned, now completely spent.

"Oh, Ada, let's get you inside," Jane said with concern. Indeed, Ada's face had taken a greenish light, and shadows formed under her eyes.

"There's still Brocklehurst to contend with," said Alice.

"One thing at a time," said Mary. The girls made their way toward the house.

The hurried hoofbeats of horses startled them, as did the rattle from a hurtling carriage.

"Miss Byron? Miss Godwin?" came a woman's voice as the carriage door popped open hurriedly.

"Mrs. Somerville!" cried Mary.

"Thank heavens you're all right," said Mrs. Somerville, who looked at Lizzie twice before realizing she wasn't Lizzie at all.

"Mrs. Somerville, this is Lizzie's twin, Alice, your cousin and our ghost. Explanations aplenty, I promise you, but after we get everyone inside!"

"Mary? Ada!" said Peebs, exiting the carriage. Behind him clambered out two short men in the dress of the city constabulary. Peebs pointed to the door of

the main house and nodded. The constables bran-
dished their gleaming black clubs and ran toward it—
just as Mr. Brocklehurst opened the front door to see
what the commotion was all about. He tried to shut
the door quickly, but the constables were upon him.

"How?" was all Mary could think to ask.

Peebs removed his own cloak and made something
of a tent for Mary and Alice as they walked to the
door. He gathered Ada in his arms, and she smiled up
at him. Jane struggled to keep up with Mrs. Somerville, who strode with purpose to the front door.

"Because I know you, Mary. I knew that when you
learned I had failed in getting a message to Lizzie that
nothing would stay you from slipping out and coming
to her aid yourself. But I knew too that Mrs. Somerville would have authority in these matters, and so I
had my attorneys—with the help of our good Master
Dickens, I might add—track down the fellows who
manage Mrs. Somerville's affairs and who might know
of her location. She was returning from what appears
to have been a wild goose chase in Scotland—a ruse,
as it turns out—and I intercepted her that I might accompany her here, with the constabulary."

"But how did you know to bring the constables?"

"Because I had every confidence that you and Ada would have the case wrapped up by the time we arrived."

"Well done, Peebs," said Ada groggily. Which meant more to him than she could ever know.

ALMOST ALL IS WELL

21

The storm had blown itself out, and the morning was bright and clear, if chilly. Mary woke to an unusual sound, that of a fire being laid for her, and she thanked the maid profusely. The maid, unaccustomed to being gushed over so, nodded uncomfortably and directed Mary to some clothes of Lizzie's that might fit her, then asked if she'd like to dress and join the others for breakfast or if she'd prefer a tray brought up.

Mary said she'd go down and quickly donned quite the prettiest dress she'd ever worn. In the dining room, Mrs. Somerville, Jane, and Peebs were at breakfast, speaking in hushed tones. They stopped when they saw her, and smiled, and rose. Mary felt a flood of relief, as she'd felt somehow that she would be in trouble, and almost burst into tears.

"There, there, Miss Godwin. All's right with the world, although the newspapers say that there's another missing patient from the hospital," Mrs. Somerville said with a wink. "Never mind, we'll get it all sorted. I will take control of the entire affair. Clearly my faith in the Wollstonecraft Detective Agency was well founded."

"Clearly," said a voice from the hall. "It's as well you didn't leave things to me, cousin." Mary turned to see a wan-looking Lizzie being led by the elbow by a grinning Allegra.

"Lizzie!" Mary cried, and rushed to help her to a seat.

"I daresay that dress suits you better than it does me."

Mary brushed her borrowed gown. "I hope you don't mind—the maid said it was—"

"Not at all! You must keep it," said Lizzie. "Allegra told me you would all be here. She told me so many things I could scarcely fathom . . . I thought it best to come home."

"Longest carriage ride ever, again," Allegra chimed in. "I thought we'd be in Wales by now, and my bum's gone numb."

Jane gasped, Peebs coughed politely, and Mrs. Somerville clucked a bemused never-mind.

"Mr. Brocklehurst is in custody, so you can rest easy here," Peebs assured Lizzie.

"What of Sir Caleb?" asked Mary.

"I imagine he's had a rather uncomfortable night. He and Brocklehurst were at each other's throats, and the constables thought it safer not to transport them together, so they left him where he was—locked up in the crypt. They should be back for him soon."

Mary sat down to her bacon and toast at last and found she was ravenous.

They spoke further, and after a second pot of tea, they were alerted by a squeaky stair to the arrival of a shaky but determined Ada, who it turned out was quite as ravenous as Mary, which quieted the worst of Mary's fears for her health.

And then, in the doorway, appeared a much-restored Alice, looking not ghostlike but perhaps a bit tentative.

Lizzie turned and the two girls stared in wonder, each feeling as if she were seeing her own reflection. Lizzie was too wobbly from her long journey to stand, but she reached out her hand and said simply, "Sister," and Alice ran into her arms.

"Welcome home, dear sister," said Lizzie. "At long last."

All together at last, each girl shared her piece of the story, filling in the gaps of information that remained.

"And what of you, Cousin Alice?" asked Mrs. Somerville. "It is you we know least of. However did you fare, once lost to the family?"

"I did not know I was lost, madam," replied Alice. "I was raised in a loving home, not so very far from here. My parents—my adoptive parents, as I know now—are both in service in Varens Manor, and it was there I met the estate manager of this house, who was conferring with the Varenses' manager."

"Bottlethirst," said Ada contemptuously.

"Mr. Brocklehurst, yes. He looked at me ever so strangely the first time we met. But then we chanced to meet in town one day, and he was quite the gentleman. He introduced me to his friend Sir Caleb, and all has been a whirl since. A baronet! And he wanted to marry me!" Alice shook her head.

But Mrs. Somerville nodded, understanding.

"And no sooner are we married than they introduced me to Papa. My real father, they say, and it gladdened my heart to know him. But he was suspicious of Sir Caleb, and when I questioned Caleb about it, he shut me up in the hospital."

"Ghastly," said Jane, who could not help herself. This time, no one stopped her.

"But I had overheard them talking," continued Alice. "I heard I had a sister, and that Caleb and Mr. Brocklehurst were going to try again. I could not stand the thought of them doing to another what they had done to me."

Alice paused from her tale. "I must thank you. Each of you. You have saved me from much wickedness, and I can never repay your kindness."

Mary took both of her hands. "Kindness is repaid by friendship, Alice."

"And I thank you as well," interrupted Lizzie, "for rescuing me from that awful hospital. After I took a chill in the rain like Ada, Mr. Brocklehurst presented me, in my delirium, as their missing patient. And there I would have remained save for the courage of all of you."

There was a knock on the door, and the butler came to alert Mrs. Somerville—who had taken command of the house at large—that the constabulary had arrived to relieve them of the prisoner. The entire household accompanied the constables along the crunching gravel path to the crypt, where a chilled and miserable Sir Caleb huddled in fear. He gave little resistance as the constables led him to believe that tea or at least a blanket would be waiting in his cell.

The constables tipped hats and muttered formalities to Peebs and Mrs. Somerville, ignoring the girls altogether, and left the lot of them on the scorched stair, which was still draped with Mary's now-ruined wool cloak.

"I can show you now. Look," Ada directed Mrs. Somerville. "It's not a tomb, it's a book. This book tells a story—a love story. A steganograph hidden in the Roman numerals. Some have these little holes, here, see, and these here, and here, aren't Roman at all, they're Greek," said Ada. "I knew that it must be some sort of code."

"It is," said Mary, feeling clever that she'd grasped Ada's solution. "And it's a testament too, Alice, of how much your parents loved and missed you. Look up."

There in the flecked silver ceiling, the Greek letters and larger Roman numerals upside down, spelled the name: A L I C E.

"Marvelous," said Mrs. Somerville. "Steganography." The girls held hands tightly.

"Wait," said Ada. Something itched in her brain. "This can't be all of it. It's too easy. I mean, it's lovely that they lie there, looking up at the name of their lost daughter, but . . ." She crept farther in the tomb, respectfully avoiding stepping on the graves, and knelt down to each letter in the cipher—first Greek, then Roman, and finally Greek again, her fingers running the channels of the inscription to the finger-poke-sized holes below. Slowly, gently, she found what she was looking for.

Pressing each of the holes rewarded her with a tiny click. When the last Greek sigma had been pressed, a rolling, clicking, sliding, stone-on-stone sound reverberated, and in the far wall, a grey panel slid away to reveal a long, narrow, silver box.

Ada smiled as the others gaped in amazement—at

the cleverness of the design and the cleverness of Ada herself. She ventured to the far wall, removed the box, and opened it to reveal a large sheet of parchment, folded upon itself multiple times and sealed with a blob of crimson wax.

The will.

A TALE IN THE LIBRARY

22

As the Londoners prepared for the journey back to town, Mary and Jane met in an upstairs hallway and noticed the half-open door to the library, just as Ada had done on their first visit. Jane pushed gently on the door and took a silent step inward, though Mary waited in the hall.

"Whatever could you possibly want of me?" said the dusty uncle, annoyed words in an unannoyed tone.

"Mr. Thorpe, I presume."

"Don't shout so, child," he said, although Jane was not shouting.

"You knew. You must have known," Jane stated quietly.

"If I knew, I don't now, whatever you're prattling on about," he said.

"A library's a good place for stories," said Jane pointedly. "How about this one? Although I'm sure you've heard it." She stilled the anger in her voice, although it held an edge as she sat down opposite the dilapidated Thorpe.

"Once there was a young couple who fell in love. Only, she was an heiress, and he a young man who had yet to make his fortune. And so her family did not approve the match."

"Nor should they have." Thorpe nodded.

"But they were married anyway, quietly, and had twin daughters."

"Enough," coughed Thorpe. "You know nothing of such things."

"But I do know, Mr. Thorpe. As do you. Church records. Orphanages. Shall I continue? It's such a sad story, it needs telling. Impoverished, they were forced to give up the girls for adoption, while our groom goes to find his fortune. Which he does, to the satisfaction of his bride's family at last. And so there is a proper

Society wedding, this time. They search for their girls but find only one, leaving a hole in both their hearts."

"A scandal, best forgotten."

"A girl, sir. A person. And because her origins were secret, she became prey for two unscrupulous men."

"Whatever are you talking about, girl? I know nothing of these matters."

"But you do—these unscrupulous men were here in your house. You approved the match of Sir Caleb and your niece."

"A baronet, yes," Thorpe said. "A good match."

"Not so good, no. A horrible man. A fortune hunter. Have you no care for your niece at all, sir?"

"Care? Don't confound me with cares, child," he rebuked. "Brocklehurst came to me with the match, and I approved. That is the entirety of my contribution."

"And on what, dare I ask, did you base such approval?"

"He was in a book. Quite reputable."

"*Burke's Peerage, Baronetage, and Knightage?*"

"That's the one."

"And on that alone you placed the fortune and future happiness of your niece?" Jane's voice wavered between contempt and disbelief. Eavesdropping from the doorway, Mary silently cheered her sister on.

"I'll not tolerate your wearisome tone, girl. What do you know of such complexities? We have standards to maintain, and you young moderns will see them overthrown, I have no doubt." He sighed heavily.

"I hope we will set better standards, sir. I hope we will see things more clearly."

The old man merely waved his hand, as if shooing a bothersome fly. And so Jane too sighed heavily and took her leave.

He was silent for a moment before conceding. "Still, it is a new century."

"It is, sir," said Jane. "It has been for the last twenty-six years."

THE CLEVEREST GIRL
IN ENGLAND

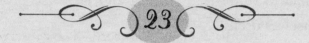

That afternoon, back at the Byron house, Ada sat propped up in bed, having been ushered there by Mrs. Woolcott, Mrs. Somerville, Anna, *and* Mary, with instructions to stay put.

Beside her lay a box of pencils, a compass, and a ruler. There were even a few scraps of paper, two books, and a discarded shawl on the floor.

Mrs. Somerville had come up to say her last thank-yous and goodbyes to an Ada already lost in her book, and she gave Mary a wink as she left.

Ada looked up when the door clicked. "You did it, Mary. You uncovered the secrets."

"Only with the dates that you left me," deferred Mary. "And you found the will!"

"Together, then," Ada said.

"Together, all of us," said Mary. Ada grimaced, but she had to admit that Allegra and Jane had proved themselves useful.

"And yet . . . ," said Ada.

"Yet what? Have I missed something?"

"So you found out," Ada asked, "how Bubbleburst knew there was a missing twin? And how he found Alice? The Jamaica connection? And how he was connected to Sir Caleb? And why he had the same kind of tattoo on his arm as the fishmonger from our first case?"

Mary froze for a moment, stunned. She hadn't found out any of these things. She didn't even realize they were questions that needed answering.

But they did remind her of another lingering question that perhaps could be answered.

She hurried downstairs, eager to catch Mrs. Somerville before her carriage departed, but was momentarily distracted by the sight of Peebs, outside in

the rain, seeing to a very large crate being swung by a crane from a wagon onto the doorstep of the Marylebone house, with two soggy workmen trying their level best to mind their language. She went to investigate.

"Peebs, what in heaven is this?" Mary asked.

"This? Something I arranged after the . . . er . . . incident with the balloon. It's finally arrived. Quicker than I thought, to be honest."

"What could it possibly be?"

"A surprise, although if you tell her, it might cheer her up. It's a steam engine, for Ada's next balloon. I thought it might be useful if she could, well, steer the next one. That and keep it aloft without anyone having to leap out of it midair." He laughed.

Mary clapped her hands in delight—the device would indeed rouse Ada's spirits. But she still had one burning question to ask, and Mrs. Somerville was climbing aboard the carriage.

"Mrs. Somerville! Mrs. Somerville! If you have a

moment!" Mary ran into the street, taking care to dodge the crane and the crate and the wagon and the workmen.

"Of course, Miss Godwin, what is it?"

"You referred to Ada as the second cleverest girl in England."

"That's right, yes. We often do, Mr. Babbage and I. She's terribly clever, your Ada."

"She is, of course she is. But then—who is the cleverest girl in England?"

Mrs. Somerville's smile faded, and Mary almost thought she saw her shiver.

"That would be Nora Radel." She paused. "May you never meet."

NOTES

1826

The year itself is practically a character in this series. John Quincy Adams was president of the United States. The prince regent of England had become King George IV just six years before, and the future Queen Victoria was only seven years old. By 1826, the world had seen a recent flurry of inventions: Volta's electric battery (1800), Fulton's submarine and torpedo (1800), Winsor's patented gas lighting (1804), Trevithick's steam locomotive (1804), Davy's electric arc light (1809), Bell's steam-powered boat (1812), and Sturgeon's electromagnet (1824). It was an exciting time of technological advancement, and it brought forth two very bright girls who changed the world through their intellect and imagination.

The lives of women—and particularly girls—were extremely limited and under constant watch. Women were not allowed to vote or practice professions, and were widely thought to be less capable than men. A girl's value to her family was in her reputation and her service, and she was expected to obediently accept a husband of her parents' choosing. Any threat to that reputation—like behaving unusually—was often enough to ruin a family.

However, because girls were not expected to have a career and compete with their (or anybody's) husband, upper-class girls were free to read or study as they wished, for few people took them seriously. Because of this rare freedom, the nineteenth century saw a sharp

surge in the intellectual contributions of female scientists and mathematicians, with Ada foremost among them.

AUGUSTA ADA BYRON (1815– 1852) was a brilliant mathematician and the daughter of the poet Lord Byron (who died when Ada was eight). Largely abandoned by her mother, she was raised by servants (and sometimes her grandmother) at the Marylebone house and was very much cut off from the world as a child.

With her legendary temper and lack of social skills (a modern historian unkindly calls her "mad as a hatter"), Ada made few friends. Her mother insisted that young Ada have no connection to her father's friends or even his interests, so Ada turned to mathematics. She worked with her friend Charles Babbage on the tables of numbers for his "Analytical Engine"—a mechanical computer— which was not built in his lifetime. But Ada's contribution to the work, as well as her idea that computers could be used not only for mathematics but also for creative works such as music, has led many people to refer to Ada as "the world's first computer programmer." Babbage called her the Enchantress of Numbers.

Ada grew to control her temper and insecurities, and was married at nineteen to William King, a baron, who became the Count of Lovelace three years later. This is why Ada is more commonly known as Ada Lovelace. She had three children—Byron,

Annabella, and Ralph—and died of cancer at the age of thirty-six. She continues to inspire scientists and mathematicians to this day, and many worthwhile projects are named after her.

MARY WOLLSTONECRAFT GODWIN (1797–1851) was the daughter of the famous feminist writer Mary Wollstonecraft (who died ten days after giving birth) and the political philosopher William Godwin. William Godwin married Mary Jane Clairmont in 1801, and Mary grew up in a mixed household of half siblings and stepsiblings in Somers Town, in what was then the northern part of London. She read broadly and had an appetite for adventure and romanticism. She ran away with Percy Shelley at age sixteen, and over one very famous weekend with Shelley, Lord Byron (Ada's father), and early vampire novelist Dr. John Polidori, Mary came up with the idea for the world's first science-fiction novel—*Frankenstein; or, The Modern Prometheus*—which she wrote at age nineteen.

In real life, Mary was eighteen years older than Ada. But I thought it would be more fun this way—to cast these two luminaries as friends.

PERCY BYSSHE (rhymes with "fish") SHELLEY (1792–1822) was an important poet and best friend to Ada's father, Lord Byron. Percy came from a wealthy family, and he offered to support Mary's father and the Godwin family. At age twenty-two, he ran off with then-sixteen-year-old Mary to Switzerland, and they were married two years later. He drowned at the age of twenty-nine when his sailboat sank in a storm.

While, in reality, Peebs had died even before our story begins, I have extended his life so that they can be in this story together. It is Peebs, as Ada's father's friend and Mary's future husband, who provides a real-life link between our two heroines.

CHARLES DICKENS (1812–1870) is considered one of the great writers of Victorian England. He really was fourteen in 1826, and he really did work in a boot-polish factory, gluing labels. He loved books and was a keen observer of everyday life in London. The bit about the carriage and pretending not to be there is made up, although he was certainly clever enough—*and* cheeky enough—to have gotten away with it. The names Gulpidge, Chowser, and Dedlock come from his writings (though Brocklehurst and Earnshaw are borrowed, with thanks, from Charlotte Brontë). He is best known to young readers as the author of *A Christmas Carol*.

Just as the first Wollstonecraft novel was in part inspired by Wilkie Collins's *The Moonstone* (1868), widely regarded as the first detective novel in English, Collins's book *The Woman in White* (1859) was a jumping-off point for this story. *The Woman in White* was the first novel to feature a female detective—a role here played by Ada. The story also includes secret twin girls, an escape from a hospital, a bored and fragile relative in a library, and a secret in a crypt. The bit about Ada being caught in the rain and contracting a fever is from Collins as well. In real life, Ada was quite sick as a young girl and was stuck in bed for almost two years.

JANE

CLARA MARY JANE CLAIRMONT (1798–1879) was known as Jane as a child but later adopted the name Claire. She really was Mary's stepsister (her mother married Mary's father), but her real life diverges dramatically from this story. Jane was actually Allegra's mother! I adjusted her timeline and role so that the two sets of sisters—Ada and Allegra, Mary and Jane—could work together as friends and detectives.

Lord Byron called Claire "a little fiend," but she referred to him as a few moments of happiness and a lifetime of trouble. She was an aspiring novelist and extremely well-read. Claire traveled throughout Europe, living in Russia for a time, returning to England to care for her mother, moving to Paris, and then finally settling in Italy. She was the longest-lived of all the Shelley-Byron circle.

ALLEGRA

CLARA ALLEGRA (Alba) **BYRON** (1817–1822) was the daughter of Claire Clairmont and Lord Byron. Her mother could not care for her, so she was left with her father. He, however, frequently left her in the care of strangers, eventually placing her in a convent in Italy. She died of fever at the age of five, but I have moved her timeline and brought her to life in the world of Wollstonecraft, to be a truer sister to Ada.

MARY SOMERVILLE (1780–1872) was a mathematician, astronomer, and feminist. She grew up in Scotland and, after being sent away to boarding school, was secretly tutored alongside her brother in mathematics. In 1831, she translated a complex algebra text into plain English for the marvelously named Society for the Diffusion of Useful Knowledge. She and Caroline Herschel were jointly nominated as the first

MRS. SOMERVILLE

female members of the Royal Astronomical Society. Somerville was also awarded a medal by the Royal Geographical Society. She wrote books on mathematics, geography, and physics, as well as molecular and microscopic science. There is both a crater on the moon and an asteroid named after her.

DR. POLIDORI

JOHN WILLIAM POLIDORI (1795–1821) was a physician, poet, and horror writer who is credited with writing the first vampire story in English. He was a good friend of both Lord Byron and Percy Shelley. As he was dead before our story takes place, his timeline has been adjusted to mesh with that of Peebs, Jane, and Mary. Because of the era's use of leeches in medicine, I have made him a bit of a vampire himself. He was an Englishman, despite his Italian name, and had an "unplaceable" accent. His eyebrows, however, were entirely terrifying.

WILLIAM GODWIN (1756–1836) was a publisher, novelist, and political thinker. Educated as a minister, he wrote books on religion and philosophy, as well as several books for children. After Mary's mother, Mary Wollstonecraft, died, Godwin honored her request to publish her diaries, even though her ideas were so different at the time that it meant people tended to be very disapproving. He and his children were often quite poor. Politically, his main idea was that poverty and crime and war could be eliminated if everyone would sit down and have a reasonable chat about things, after which there would be very little need for things like government.

MARY GODWIN

MARY (Marie) **JANE CLAIRMONT GODWIN** (1766–1841) was the mother of Jane and the wife of Mary's father, William Godwin, which makes her Mary's stepmother. Little is known about her early life, which is to say that the story she told everyone seems to have been completely made up. But we do know that at one point she was living with her children in the Polygon next to Godwin and his daughters after the death of his first wife. She seems to have decided to marry Godwin and pretty much talked him into it, leaving him little choice. She was known to have a temper, to choose favorites among her children (always Jane and never Mary), and to be levelheaded about money and business. She was the most successful publisher of children's literature in England at the time.

THE POLYGON

The Polygon was a fifteen-sided apartment building in Clarendon Square in Somers Town, in what was then the northern part of London (the city has long since grown around it). It was home not only to the Godwin family, but later to Charles Dickens. Dickens wrote about the Polygon, making it the home of Harold Skimpole in the novel *Bleak House*. Scholars have speculated that the character of Skimpole may have been based on William Godwin. While the building is long gone, the road that bears its name remains.

Join the
Wollstonecraft
Detectives
on their next case!

Turn the page for a sneak peek at Book Three,
The Case of the Counterfeit Criminals.

QED

Rain spattered forcefully against Ada's window. The sound merged with the shushing in her ears, mashed as they were against the pillows that propped her up in bed. It was difficult reading only with her right hand, but she was making good progress turning the page with her thumb, though it made her wrist ache. This took her mind away from the wet, black, squirming creatures embedded in her left arm, slowly drinking her blood.

Her book was also a refuge from the stranger who sat at her bedside. The man gave her a chill whenever she thought of him, let alone looked at him, with his pale complexion and dark caterpillar eyebrows.

That's not fair, Ada admitted to herself. Now that she was on the doorstep of her twelfth birthday, she was trying to be more grown-up about this sort of thing. She knew her aversion to strangers, to new things, wasn't entirely rational. And the man was, she supposed, not entirely a stranger, despite his strangeness. Dr. Polidori had been a friend of her father's, the father she scarcely knew. And he'd been there, day after tedious day, draining away her blood in small munching gulps from his little pets—the leeches he would gently pluck away with steel forceps and place in their glass jar when he was done.

"Almost there," said the doctor in his strange, unplaceable accent, as though sensing Ada's discomfort. "We must purge the fevered blood."

"One would think," said Ada, meaning herself, "that someone with no blood would be dead, and someone with blood would be more likely to be alive."

"That is the case, yes," said Dr. Polidori slowly.

"Therefore, more blood is better than less blood, QED," declared Ada. "That's Latin, *quod erat demonstrandum,* meaning 'thus it is proven.'"

"Your Latin is excellent, Lady Ada," the doctor acknowledged distantly, teasing away the leeches with his long steel instrument and dabbing the leftover drops of blood on her arm.

"Mmm," she said. "Then why are you taking blood out of me?"

"You suffered a terrible fever," the doctor declared. "This poisons the blood, which must be removed for you to regain your . . . vitality." He savored the final word in a way that made Ada queasy. But she was often queasy after her leechings.

"Not all my blood, surely," Ada said.

"Merely the fevered blood." Ada again queased at the way he said "blood," like he'd dropped his tongue on a tiled floor, the word easing and then flopping in his mouth.

"How can they tell? The leeches, I mean. How do they know fevered blood from good blood?"

The doctor continued restoring the black worms to their jar. "Such is a mystery of nature."

"It's the sort of thing someone ought to be figuring out."

Polidori said nothing.

"I mean," Ada continued, "there you are, a little

leech, happily lapping up fevered blood, and then you find a spot of perfectly ordinary, good blood. Do you say *Ugh, no thank you, I couldn't possibly*? I don't see it happening. Honestly, there ought to be some sort of evidence. . . ."

Just then, Ada's bedroom door clicked open. Gravity and old hinges let the door drift slowly and ghostlike to the wall of its own accord, and in cartwheeled Ada's nine-year-old half sister, Allegra, still in her nightdress.

The girl thrust her arms above her head in a silent *ta-da!* pose, curls bouncing around her face, until she caught sight of Dr. Polidori.

"Aaaaack!" Allegra said, and hurried out of the room.

"Allegra is not fond of leeches," said Ada to Polidori, who again said nothing.

INTRACTABLES

An hour later, Ada had breakfasted and wiggled wearily into her cherry velvet gown, and made her way to the drawing room in search of a newspaper. She smiled at her best friend, Mary, who stood and gave Ada's hand a squeeze. Mary's stepsister, Jane, stood and gave a halfhearted curtsy. Allegra stayed seated in an overstuffed chair, books at her feet unopened, scone crumbs scattered down her morning dress.

The girls' tutor, Peebs, opened his rain-wet leather case and began extracting books, nodding and smiling at the girls. It was not a particularly talkative morning, how-do-you-dos apparently having been satisfied downstairs, before Ada's arrival.

Despite it being a grand room for a grand house, the sprawl of girls and books and tutor made the drawing room seem almost cramped. Ada, still tired from her daily leeching, retreated behind a grey wall of newsprint to survey the *Times* and see what was going on in the world beyond the stately townhouse in Marylebone.

In truth, Ada was only half-reading, or perhaps reading with half her brain. When the reading half paused to see what the other half had been up to, it continued reading, because what the other half had, in fact, been up to was writing. Ada had written a name in pencil, right there in the pages of the *Times*.

Nora Radel.

Mary Somerville, the smartest woman in the whole world and the Wollstonecraft Detective Agency's last client, had said that Nora Radel was the cleverest girl in all of England.

Which made Ada the second cleverest. And, therefore, the most curious.

Who was this mysterious girl? Why had Ada's friend and mathematical mentor, Mr. Babbage, who reportedly knew this Nora person, never mentioned her before? Exactly how much cleverer was she than Ada herself, and in what way? The whole thing was driving her mad, or would be if she'd had the energy. But the leeches had drained her, so she was mostly just woozy. Despite all her researches, she'd found no trace of Nora Radel.

Down the hall in her room, in the midst of a stack of books Ada could picture perfectly, lay a notebook entitled "Intractables," which contained a series of questions Ada could not pose to her Byron Lignotractatic Engine, or "bleh" for short. The bleh was a large brass calculating contraption of her own invention. It could take into account dozens of factors in a problem via a set of spindles and sprockets, and then clack along until a pattern appeared, which Ada would read as a solution. Or at least a different starting point.

The bleh was very good for keeping track of things with numbers, like how often a white horse could be seen in the road between the hours of ten and eleven each morning. It could take in the number of times the newspaper reported burglaries involving portraits, and it could even show relationships between the two sets of numbers (horses and burglaries). Even nun sightings, which Allegra had insisted were worth keeping track of.

But, as yet, the bleh was not particularly good at understanding the patterns of *people*. Such unexpected things she kept track of in her intractables notebook, as there was simply no quantifying them.

Nora Radel was such an intractable. Even though Ada had set a spindle aside for her, there were few variables defined, no way of putting the pegs in the holes that made any sense: Girl, yes. London, yes. Clever, yes. Cleverer than me, (a reluctant) yes. Known to Mr. Babbage and Mrs. Somerville, yes.

Not much to work with.

And, she had to admit, not much reason to care. She'd had little time for the bleh these past weeks. She had a dirt map to finish and a hot-air balloon to rebuild. Yet care she did.

"Kingdom, phylum, class, order, family, genus, species," said Peebs, beginning his lecture. "Keeping precious creatures organized for grumpy scientists," he finished, laughing at his own joke. None of the girls responded in any way.

"Ah," he concluded. "Right, then."

"Taxonomy," said Ada, not looking up from her newspaper.

"Precisely," said Peebs.

"I'm terribly sorry," interjected Mary. "But I haven't a clue as to what you're going on about. Perhaps if—"

"Not a word," interrupted Jane.

"Nope," said Allegra. "Start over."

"Taxonomy," Ada repeated. "It's how you organize animals, how you name them."

"Precisely," said Peebs. "Thank you, Lady Ada. In this way we can categorize all manner of animal in the world—including humans."

"Humans are not animals," snipped Jane.

"I'm afraid we are, Miss Jane," countered Peebs.

"I'm an animal," volunteered Allegra cheerfully.

"Circus chimp," suggested Ada from the recesses of her newspaper.

Peebs rolled his eyes, and Mary was about to intervene when she noticed a number of things in quick succession.

First, through the open door she noticed Mrs. Woolcott, Ada's former governess and current fever-nurse, walking down the corridor, toward the stairs. Next, she noticed Mr. Franklin, Ada's extraordinarily

tall and ever-silent butler, coming up the stairs with what appeared to be an overflowing letters-tray. This was unusual, as the girls had had almost no letters in recent weeks. And, most curiously of all, she noticed a silent exchange between Mrs. Woolcott and Mr. Franklin, in which Mrs. Woolcott offered a very clear "no" with the shake of her head, gathered the bundle of letters, and headed down the hallway toward the library.

When her attention returned to the drawing room, Mary was startled to see Ada staring directly at her.

"What?" said Ada.

"What what, Ada?"

"What you were noticing what, Mary. I notice when you notice things. I'm getting quite good at it."

All eyes were on Mary now.

"Is everything all right, Miss Mary?" Peebs asked.

"I just . . . It seems that . . . Well, I believe there is correspondence," said Mary, uncomfortably on the spot.

"Correspondence," said Ada, folding her newspaper. She looked quickly around the room.

"Library," Ada announced. "Now."

A PURELY THEORETICAL EXERCISE

"Absolutely not," said Mrs. Woolcott.

"Mrs. Woolcott, I'm certain—" Mary began.

"We are all of us certain of precisely one thing, Miss Godwin, and that is that Dr. Polidori has made it very clear that Lady Ada is to be allowed out of bed for meals and brief tutoring only," insisted Mrs. Woolcott. She had turned from clicking the key in a cabinet to spy a gaggle of girls at the library door, insisting on seeing the newly arrived letters.

"Miss Coverlet—" Ada began.

"It is Mrs. Woolcott now, Lady Ada," corrected Mrs. Woolcott.

"Fine. But those are my letters," Ada said crossly.

"Ours, to be perfectly frank," said Jane, and a little whirring click in the counters of Ada's brain noticed that it was a rather rude tone for Jane to be taking.

Ada went to plop herself in her favorite high-backed chair when she stopped suddenly.

"What have you done with my chair?"

"Nothing at all, Lady Ada; it is right there in front of you," Mrs. Woolcott assured.

"It's not. It's got the wrong all everything."

"I had the cushion reupholstered, if that is what you are referring to."

Ada gave it a poke with a finger and made a face.

Mary and Allegra shot each other a she-shouldn't-have-done-that look, thinking of poor Mrs. Woolcott. Everything was silent for the briefest of moments while Ada sucked in all the air from the room.

"MR. FRANKLINNNN!" Ada bellowed.

It was as though he had been standing there the entire time, invisible, and only now materialized. The butler loomed in the doorframe, silent and expressionless.

"I need my chair from the drawing room. And get rid of . . . that." She waved vaguely in the direction of the library chair.

"Please," whispered Mary.

"Please," Ada repeated.

"Mrs. Woolcott," Mary intervened. "Lady Ada will be seated presently, and tucked in with a blanket if you like. Reading her correspondence would hardly be more taxing than undertaking her studies."

"It is not reading the correspondence that concerns me," said Mrs. Woolcott. "It's what comes after. Eavesdropping in thunderstorms. Breaking into hospitals. Running off to crypts at all hours . . ."

"Perhaps," Mary added as Mr. Franklin arrived with the overstuffed and un-reupholstered chair from the drawing room, "if Ada read her mail as a purely theoretical exercise . . ."

"What's 'theoretical'?" asked Allegra.

"Thinking," said Mary, smiling. "A thinking-only sort of exercise. A puzzle to be solved in a very relaxing, sitting-down, not-taking-any-action sort of way."